DOCTOR IN NEW GUINEA

A novel

Dana James

Published by Accent Press Ltd – 2013
ISBN 9781909840881

Chapter One

Dr Maren Harvey kicked off her sandals, walked barefoot across the wooden floor to the window and looked out on to the exotic flowering shrubs and tall palms surrounding the small, single-storey hotel.

Her sleeveless cotton dress clung damply as she lifted the curtain of dark glossy hair off her neck and revelled in the deliriously cool air whispering across her skin.

The mountain ranges of the Eastern Highlands, swathed in lush tropical forest, rose into the blue sky only a few hundred yards away. Even as she watched, puffs of white cloud, like cotton wool balls, tumbled over the mountain peaks, heralding the inevitable rain which fell late every afternoon.

This was Papua New Guinea, the world's largest tropical island, three-quarters of it untouched by civilisation.

Maren's skin tightened with a small shiver of excitement. Soon she would be setting off into those mountains.

During the past four years spent in malaria research at the Hospital for Tropical Diseases in London, she had never dreamed that one day she would have the opportunity to get out of the laboratory and actually see for herself the conditions which produced the disease. This, her first field trip, had been Russell's idea. It was going to be the adventure of a lifetime.

Maren breathed in deeply. Though the air here in the mountains was as warm as high summer in England, it tasted like nectar compared with the stifling humidity of the island's capital, Port Moresby, where she had landed that morning.

Reluctantly, Maren turned away from the window. She wanted to freshen up and change her creased and travel-weary dress before meeting Russell to make the final arrangements. She felt as excited as a schoolgirl, which at 26 was nothing short of ridiculous.

As she lifted her suitcase onto the bed, Maren recalled the brown-skinned porter's smiling but definite refusal of her proffered tip. A small card on the back of the door, unnoticed when she had entered, caught her eye, and she paused to read it.

FRIENDLY AND COURTEOUS SERVICE IS A PAPUA NEW GUINEA TRADITION AND GRATUITIES FOR WHAT COMES NATURALLY ARE NOT EXPECTED

This was an unusual country in more ways than she had expected.

The telephone buzzed softly, its gleaming white plastic completely out of place among the natural wood, muted earthy colours and traditional designs on the rugs and bedcover. Maren pushed her suitcase aside and sat down on the bed, drawing her long legs under her as she picked up the receiver.

'Hello, this is Dr Harvey.'

'Maren, my dear, it's me.' The rich tones of

Professor Russell Brent's voice echoed clearly down the line.

A fond smile curved Maren's full lips as a vivid picture of the short, rotund figure she had known since childhood sprang into her mind.

'Oh, Russell, I can hardly believe I'm actually here.' She could barely contain her excitement. 'And I know if it wasn't for you, I wouldn't be. Did you have to pull many strings on my behalf?'

'Not a single one,' he laughed. 'Your research results were recommendation enough. Did you have a good journey?'

Once more Maren freed the damp hair clinging to her neck. 'I seem to have been travelling for ever. I've lost track of the days.'

'It's Monday,' Brent put in helpfully.

'Well, I left London on Saturday evening, arrived in Hong Kong on Sunday evening, just had time to change planes, and we got to Port Moresby at six-thirty this morning.'

'I suppose you had a bit of a wait in the capital?'

She appreciated the sympathy. 'Eight hours.'

'You will have found it rather hot.'

'A little,' she agreed drily. 'It was like breathing treacle. I was glad to reach Goroka. Russell, about the trip –'

'How are your parents?' he cut in, appearing not to have heard her.

'They're fine. Father's in Zurich at the moment. Business will keep him there for several weeks so Mother went with him.' Maren hitched herself higher up the bed and leaned against the headboard. 'Then they're going on to New York. They expect to be back in England to spend Christmas with Lucy and George and the children.'

'How is life treating our tame aristocrat?'

'Russell,' Maren scolded, 'you make him sound like some rare animal.'

'My dear girl, a marquis who can run a stately home and estate at a profit in these stringent times is indeed a rare creature, believe me,' Brent replied. 'Are Lucy and the brats well?'

The reference to her sister and children made Maren smile again. 'They're fine. Christopher starts at Eton next year and the two girls are already terrorising the local Pony Club. As for Lucy –' Maren's voice softened '– I've never seen anyone so utterly content. Despite all the demands on them both, she and George seem to be on a permanent honeymoon.'

'Do I detect a note of envy?' Brent's tone was light.

'No, you don't. I'm a dedicated career girl,' Maren retorted a little too quickly.

'No one could doubt it. But I have wondered in recent months whether your dedication to your research hasn't removed you a little too far from the rest of the human race.'

'Russell, I've already got one mother. I don't need another.' Maren knew her laugh was too bright, too brittle. 'I adore my job. Working on a malaria vaccine is not only fascinating, it's vital. I'm simply too busy for distractions.' Becoming aware of the ache in her knuckles she release tight grip on the phone and flexed her fingers.

In some respects she was closer to Brent than to

her parents. But she could not reveal, even to him, the fear that fluttered inside her like the wings of a dark bird.

'Besides,' she went on quickly, swallowing the dryness in her throat. 'If I hadn't been so dedicated this trip would not have come about. And there's no other place on earth I'd rather be at this moment.' The crisis had passed. She was firmly in control again. 'Please don't keep me in suspense. When do we leave and where exactly are we going?'

There was a silence.

'You did mention the upland valleys in your letter,' she went on. 'Are there aid stations there? Or … Russell? Are you still on the line? Hello?'

'I'm still here.' His voice came back as strong as before. 'Maren, there's no way to break this gently. I'm afraid I can't make the trip.'

It was Maren's turn to be silent. She was stunned, devastated. 'Can't make it? But – but …' She couldn't believe it, didn't want to believe it. Not after all the months of planning, of waiting. After all the arrangements she'd needed to make at work to ensure experiments were covered, results noted, reports drafted. All the red tape and last-minute details. No, it couldn't be true.

'Russell, I don't understand.' She gripped the phone with both hands, sitting bolt upright as tension, anger and utter desolation chased one another. 'When did – why didn't you let me know sooner? I've come all this way …' She broke off while she could still control her voice. Her throat was stiff and aching.

'Of course you did. This is exactly where you should be.' Brent spoke with exaggerated patience. 'I didn't say *you* weren't going. I said *I* couldn't make it.'

'Then how –'

'If you will give me a chance I'll explain. I have to go to America for a World Health Organisation conference. It's related to funding. It's a chore but one I cannot escape. I've arranged that you join a colleague of mine who has a research trip of his own arranged. He's a lecturer at the Faculty of Medicine both at Port Moresby and here in Goroka. The purpose of his trip is to collect follow-up data on a disease which only occurs in one group of people living in the Eastern Highlands.'

In spite of her disappointment Maren's interest was immediately caught. 'Won't he object to me suddenly being dumped on him?'

'He owes me a favour,' Brent replied. 'Now I must go, I have a plane to catch.'

Panic surged. Once he put the phone down her only contact in this alien country would be broken.

'Russell, wait. Where – I mean, what's his name?'

'His name is Nicholas Calder. He'll meet you in the lobby of your hotel at six-thirty this evening. Now I really must go. Enjoy your trip, Maren. I think you'll discover you have a lot in common. And this trip will be one you'll never forget.'

'Don't hang up,' Maren shouted frantically. 'What does he look like? How will I know him?'

'He's 36 years old, white, and an academic. How could you miss him?' Brent's cryptic reply was tinged with a hint of laughter. But absorbed in her chaotic thoughts, Maren didn't have time to wonder why. 'Goodbye, my dear. I'll be in touch.'

There was a click and Maren was left staring at the disconnected phone.

Slowly she replaced the receiver. So, 36, white, and an academic. Well, that was clear enough, if lacking in detail. She did a mental check of the men she knew who fitted that description. There were three in the lab.

Charles in Immunology was five feet six inches tall and, if she was being tactful, on the plump side. With his rosy complexion, high forehead and rapidly receding hairline, he reminded Maren of an earnest gnome.

Then there was Guy from Haematology. She had always imagined that someone with a name like that would be a strapping rugby player or rowing blue. But though Guy was, at five feet ten, exactly the same height as her, not by any stretch of the imagination could he be termed husky, as he tried self-consciously to disguise his acne scars beneath long hair, a beard and moustache.

The only other man who fulfilled those criteria was William. Though he topped six feet, he was thin to the point of emaciation and walked with a pronounced stoop, like a sapling bowed by the breeze. He wore thin, wire-rimmed glasses, and his fair hair flopped over his forehead and collar looking as though it had been cut with a knife and fork.

They were not only her colleagues, they were her good friends, caring deeply, as she did, about their work, often assisting each other with experiments, working late into the night. She was at ease with them. As she scrambled from the bed and lifted her toilet bag out of her suitcase, the image she formed of

Nicholas Calder was a mixture of those three.

Cool and refreshed from her shower, she put on a deceptively simple long sleeveless dress of crinkle cotton. The blue and green colour mixture suited her dark hair and emphasised the luminous green of her eyes. A fine gold thread through the fabric caused it to shimmer as she moved, and a gold belt and matching sandals completed the outfit.

Her only jewellery was her watch, a slim model from Cartier, her 21st birthday present from her parents.

She brushed her hair till it gleamed, then quickly twisted it into a coil on top of her head. Though the heat had lessened as evening approached and the rain had begun to fall, she wanted to remain as cool as possible.

It was too hot for make-up, not that she ever wore much. But a critical glance in the mirror revealed the strain and demands the last year's work had made upon her. Slight shadows under her eyes, the skin drawn a fraction tight across her high cheekbones, and a slight pallor beneath her light tan.

It was just the travelling, she told herself firmly. Anyone was entitled to look pale after flying halfway across the world. For her ego's sake she applied a soft rose gloss to her mouth, closed the tube and dropped it into her evening bag. Straightening her spine she lifted her chin, closed her eyes, and inhaled then and released three slow breaths. It was a trick she had picked up during university days to combat her chronic shyness and unease at meeting strangers.

The mirror reflected an image of serene confidence. She gave it a nod, took a final deep breath

8

then left her room. After locking the door she walked along the passage with an elegance born of childhood ballet and deportment lessons. The insistence of her mother and her teachers that she be proud of her height and never, ever seek to minimise it had been a hard lesson, but it was one she had learned.

The lobby was deserted. Even the smiling receptionist who had so warmly welcomed her seemed temporarily to have vanished.

Glancing at her watch Maren saw it was a couple of minutes after six-thirty. Obviously Dr Calder had been delayed, perhaps by the rain, now falling in a relentless torrent.

There was no point in returning to her room so she wandered over to look at the display in the small shop and was immediately entranced by the wood carvings and brilliantly plumed head-dresses on sale. Pottery and basketwork lay beside woven and beaded headbands, belts and necklaces.

Dresses and shirts of soft, butter-yellow cotton printed with traditional designs in red, brown and black were arranged at one side. One in particular caught her attention. As she moved closer to examine it the outside door crashed open. She swung round, startled by the noise.

He stood at least six feet four. The short-sleeved jacket of his beige safari suit stretched tightly across massive shoulders as he shook the rain from a huge umbrella and tossed it into the stand. Raindrops glistened in his black hair and on his deeply tanned arms. His gaze raked the lobby, stopped at Maren, and she was shaken to the core by the icy disdain that spread slowly across his chiselled features.

Chapter Two

Oh no. Not him. It couldn't be him. She had never seen a man so aggressively masculine. His physical impact exploded her imaginary picture of a 36-year-old, white academic into a thousand fragments.

There was something predatory about him, an aura more suited to a hunter or explorer than a medical lecturer. Perhaps that's what he was and she had jumped to the wrong conclusion. She desperately hoped so.

But as he came towards her, his lithe strides covering the floor as smoothly and silently as a leopard, the horrible sinking feeling in her stomach told her differently.

'I'm Nicholas Calder,' he said abruptly, his voice gravel and steel. 'You, I presume, are Maren Harvey?'

Maren tilted her chin a fraction higher. Whatever had caused his obvious bad temper she had no intention of being his scapegoat. Instinct warned her that this man judged by his own standards and made no allowances.

The strong and instant antagonism between them was undeniable. It was equally obvious that the disadvantages were all on her side, though she had no idea why.

'I am Dr Harvey, yes,' Maren replied coolly, extending her hand as she met his cold gaze.

His brown eyes, so dark as to be almost black, were hooded as they swept over her and Maren knew that no detail of her appearance had escaped that fleeting scrutiny. Heavy brows met in a frown above an aquiline nose. Deep creases were scored on either side of a surprisingly sensual mouth set in an uncompromising line above a lean hard jaw.

His face and neck, down to the black hair that curled in the "v" of the immaculate beige safari jacket, were tanned mahogany. The evenness of his colour told Maren that it would be the same all over his body. She felt herself grow hot at the unexpected intimacy of that thought.

He shook her hand, reluctantly it seemed, and the contact though firm was brief. 'I suggest we eat straight away. Unless you want a drink first?'

As an invitation it left a lot to be desired. The inflection in his tone made Maren's hackles rise. She rarely touched alcohol. But after the frenetic activity of the past week and two days of non-stop travelling she had looked forward on her first evening in Papua New Guinea to a leisurely meal preceded by a glass of wine.

But the prospect of trying to make polite conversation over a drink with this terse forbidding man was not appealing. 'No, thank you. I'm quite happy to eat now.'

Without another word he turned and led the way into the dining room. They were the first diners to arrive and were greeted by a smiling waiter who led them to a corner table. The walls of the low-ceilinged room were split bamboo, the floor polished wood. A huge fan set in the ceiling stirred the air and wall lights with leaflike shades cast a soft glow over the room.

Arrangements of exotic flowers with petals of crimson, gold, purple and ivory amid lush green foliage stood on carved wooden pedestals against the walls. The tablecloths were crisp and spotless, and ice cubes tinkled in the jug of crystal water brought by the white-shirted waiter. In the background the constant drum and hiss of the tropical rain provided its own music.

The meal of chicken and pineapple served on a bed of fluffy rice with side dishes of baby onions, tomatoes, peas and green beans, looked appetising and smelled delicious. But what should have been enjoyable wasn't, because of the cold detachment of the man opposite.

He ate quickly, without fuss or ostentation, as though food were merely a fuel, not a pleasure over which to linger. She tried several times to start a conversation, commenting on the rain and the exotic flowers, but he barely glanced up, his replies becoming brief and more impatient. After the third rebuff Maren had had enough.

Putting down her knife and fork, she leaned slightly towards him. 'Dr Calder, I don't understand how it can have happened as we met barely half an hour ago. But something about me seems to have upset you. Perhaps you'd be good enough to tell me what it is so that we may sort it out and proceed to discussing the field trip.'

'That is exactly the problem,' he growled. 'How can I possibly take someone like you into the dangers of a tropical forest?'

Maren stared at him, startled. 'What do you mean someone like me?'

He gestured with one hand and sighed impatiently.

Maren glanced down at herself, then back at him. 'You can't be serious. I had not intended trekking into the jungle dressed like this.'

'That's not what I meant.' His reply was brusque. 'When I agreed with Professor Brent that a female colleague of his should accompany me, I had no idea – I expected someone very different.'

'Oh, is that so?' Maren queried sweetly. 'Well, as I am neither responsible for, nor interested in your preconceptions, perhaps you'll tell me precisely what it is about me that you object to.'

'You're too thin for a start.' His gaze was critical. 'You don't look as though you have much stamina. Are you fully aware of the physical demands an expedition like this will make on you? You've not had time to get used to the heat and humidity and I want to leave tomorrow.'

'I assure you I'm very fit. I've travelled a lot and adjust very quickly,' Maren retorted. 'Had I been a couple of stone heavier no doubt you'd be concerned about my heart and blood pressure. I promise you, you need not worry on my account.'

'I'm not,' he snapped. 'My concern is for myself. I have a job to do and I've no time to waste nursing along someone who can't keep up.' He glanced at her. 'Why are you here anyway?'

'What do you mean?' Maren was puzzled.

'I can't help wondering why you've chosen to risk your health and safety in a place like this.' A biting edge crept into his voice, 'Especially with a background like yours.'

Maren froze. *Here we go again.* But though bitter anger raced hot through her veins, her voice was calm and level.

'I also have a job to do, Dr Calder.'

He scrutinised her as though she were an object that had caught his eye, but that on closer examination he had decided to reject. 'Mmm, why medicine, though? I thought girls with your background usually ran boutiques or did the odd bit of charity work between parties.' The derision in his voice stung like a whiplash. 'I'd have thought Harley Street would have provided a better hunting ground than a place like this. Or is this trip just for kicks, a taste of the exotic before you scuttle back home to raise horses and children in a large country house, with, of course, a Mayfair flat, and a cottage on the coast, all courtesy of some chinless wonder who will use Daddy's money to keep you in the manner to which you are accustomed.'

His open contempt roused Maren to fury. 'Of all the insufferable, offensive, egotistical bigots it has been my misfortune to meet, you, Dr Calder, take first prize.' Her voice shook with rage. 'Twice you have referred to "someone like" me. You know absolutely nothing about the person I am. You have jumped to conclusions, totally false ones, based purely on my family background, over which I had no control, and your own prejudice.'

Her face was burning as her heart hammered

wildly beneath the thin cotton. Never before had she spoken to anyone like that. There had never been reason to. But Nicholas Calder's brutal jibes had so incensed her that her shyness was ignored, and good manners forgotten.

'Yes, I was born with the proverbial silver spoon in my mouth.' She kept her voice low. This was between them. 'I wasn't given the opportunity of choosing my parents. Though I've no doubt you won't believe it, money often presents as many problems as it solves. You trust people and think of them as friends, only to discover you're nothing more than a passport to better things.'

'Poor little rich girl,' Nicholas murmured sarcastically. 'Come on, surely–'

'Be quiet,' Maren hissed heedless of the consequences. 'You've aired your opinions. Have the courtesy to let me finish.'

He gave a slight shrug and gestured for her to continue. Paradoxically, this defused some of Maren's tension which made her even more annoyed.

'I refuse to apologise for my background. I've always believed that good fortune demands repayment. I was born with a lot of advantages. And I chose a career that would enable me to help other people.'

'How noble,' a cynical smile touched the corners of his mouth.

Maren leaned forward oblivious to everything but the hard, mocking expression of the dark man opposite. 'I did not buy my qualifications, Dr Calder. I worked bloody hard for them. No short cuts, no favours. I got a first at Cambridge then I went to St

Thomas's before starting research at the Hospital for Tropical Diseases in London.'

Maren sat back. Her breathing was ragged and her hands trembled so much she clasped them together on her lap. But she did not flinch from Nicholas Calder's penetrating gaze. 'I won't dignify your insinuations by denying them. I am fit and healthy. I have sound scientific reasons for being here, and my work is important and necessary. So if you are looking for a way out of taking me along, at least have the decency and the courage to be honest about it.'

She smoothed her napkin on her lap, using the unnecessary movement to help her regain control. That was it, she thought miserably. She had blown it. He would flatly refuse to take her now. Why had she allowed him to provoke her like that? She had met dozens like him, convinced that any girl with money had a head stuffed with cotton wool instead of brains.

No, she hadn't, she corrected herself. She had never met *anyone* like him: so arrogant, so self-assured, so deliberately, infuriatingly smug.

'All right, I'll take you.' He was brisk.

Maren's head came up. 'What?' She was so surprised the word slipped out before she could stop it.

'I said I'll take you,' he repeated impatiently. 'You passed. Would you like dessert? The fresh fruit cocktail is particularly good.'

'Yes, thank you.' Maren was stunned. Had he offered her cyanide her reply would have been the same. She pressed the groove between her brows, trying to release the tightness, her heart still pounding unevenly.

16

'I passed? Do you mean all that –' she gestured '– was some sort of test?'

He nodded. Then as the waiter cleared the debris of their main course, he ordered two dishes of fruit, with coffee to follow.

'It's grown locally,' he informed her.

'What is?' Maren was still trying to absorb what he'd said to her.

'The coffee, and the fruit of course. But coffee is now an important cash crop in PNG. Would you like a brandy?'

The cynical mocking man of a few moments ago had vanished, replaced by an urbane if enigmatic host.

Maren nodded wordlessly. For the first time in her life, she felt she really needed a drink.

Nothing more was said until the dishes, piled with slices of chilled tropical fruits, were placed in front of them. Maren turned her spoon between her fingers. 'Why?' she asked quietly.

Nicholas selected a piece of mango then glanced across at her. 'Spending several weeks in remote areas of the mountains and forest, the greater part of it alone, is going to make heavy demands on us both. I had to make sure you were up to it.'

'But I told you –' Maren began.

'I know what you *told* me,' he cut across her, his irritation plain. 'I prefer to find out for myself. I needed to see the person behind the façade, your weaknesses and strengths, how you stand up under pressure. Our lives could depend on it. Your reactions to my –' his mouth twitched '– let's call them "observations" revealed a hell of a lot more than you

17

would have volunteered.'

She stared unseeingly at her dish, anger battling with logic at his trickery. She had to concede he had a point. Of course he needed to know if she would be dependable in an emergency. But how could he have learned that from the scene he had just provoked? She would swear it had been no act on his part. His biting sarcasm and mocking contempt had been far too convincing. Anger burned and doubt continued to nag. What had been his real motive?

Then she realised what had just said. '*In remote areas of the mountains and forest, the greater part of it alone ...*'

Busy with her fruit she was able to avoid his dark, probing gaze. She kept her voice carefully expressionless.

'I was under the impression we would be staying either at missions in the region or at aid stations.'

'That might have been Professor Brent's plan. But my investigations will take me much further into the uninhabited regions between tribal groups. It shouldn't make any difference to the collection of your research material.' He paused, a laconic grin twisting his mouth. 'Unless the thought of being alone with me for a month bothers you?'

Instantly Maren retreated behind a veneer of cool sophistication. A furious retort sprang to her lips but she held it back. He had pierced her protective armour once. He had deliberately manipulated her into betraying doubts and hurts she had never before revealed to a living soul. She was determined it would not happen again.

She lifted her head, her gaze level and direct.

'Your ego is showing again, Dr Calder. Why should it bother me? We both have a job to do. We happen, through circumstances, to be travelling together.' She shrugged lightly. 'I'm sure neither of us would have chosen this arrangement, but let's not exaggerate its importance.'

His mouth compressed and his eyes gleamed for an instant. 'That was certainly not my intention, Dr Harvey,' he said gravely.

Maren had the uncomfortable feeling he was laughing at her. She dismissed it quickly. He had agreed she should travel with him. That was all that mattered.

Though she would have to depend on his knowledge of the region and its people, she intended to make quite sure that all contact between them remained strictly professional.

Because if she were completely honest, and though she would cut out her tongue sooner than admit it, Nicholas Calder terrified her. He was so self-contained, so arrogantly self-confident. His powerful, uncompromising maleness both attracted and frightened her, and she was not at all sure that she could trust him. Yet she had no alternative.

He reminded her of a panther she had seen in a circus once. Sleek and handsome, it appeared almost tame as it obeyed the commands of its trainer. But when the big cat lifted its head, its golden eyes gleamed with the burning, unquenchable spirit of the wild. There was something of that untameability about Nicholas Calder. He wore the cloak of civilised social behaviour with ease. But behind the bland, urbane exterior, she was aware of an elemental force that unnerved her.

She had not reached the age of 26 without learning something about men and her own reactions to them.

In her second year at university she had fallen deeply in love. He'd been doing a postgraduate year for his PhD. She had been totally absorbed by him, deaf to the kindly warnings of her classmates, blind to the truth which everyone else had recognised.

When it had ended, she'd thrown herself into her studies with single-minded determination. The experience had left deep scars. Now wary and suspicious she had encased herself in a shell of polite friendliness that kept all but a chosen few at a distance.

Nicholas Calder had cracked that shell. He had probed, found her vulnerable. She had papered over the crack but both knew it was there. How was she to cope with him, and the conflicting emotions he aroused?

She lifted the brandy balloon and gently swirled the spirit, vowing he would never know of the turmoil beneath her poise.

Nicholas set down his empty glass. 'When you're ready we'll go through to the lounge. I think it's time we got down to the details. We are leaving for Okapa at eight tomorrow morning.'

His businesslike attitude enabled Maren to relax for the first time that evening. This was the reason she had come. They were almost on their way. She felt her pulse quicken with excitement.

It was after nine when Nicholas bade her goodnight in the lobby. 'Remember you'll be carrying your own gear for at least part of the journey, so keep it to bare essentials. I hope you've brought the right kind of clothes.'

'A waterproof cape, long-sleeved cotton shirts, cotton trousers, several pairs of cotton and wool socks and ankle-high walking boots.' Maren ticked the items off on her fingers, mentally thanking Russell for warning her that denim jeans and man-made fibres were totally wrong for the conditions she would encounter.

He nodded briefly. 'I'll pick you up here at seven-thirty. Don't spend hours messing about tonight. Get to bed early and make sure you have a good breakfast in the morning.' He added, 'It will be a very long day and you aren't acclimatised yet.'

Gritting her teeth at his peremptory tone, Maren reminded herself he knew this country. She did not. But did he have to be quite so bossy?

'Goodnight, Dr Calder,' she said sweetly. 'I'll try to remember all your instructions.'

'Goodnight, Dr Harvey,' he replied, 'I have no doubt you'll succeed.' His face was expressionless, but the glint in his dark eyes warned Maren she was on dangerous ground.

She stared at the door as it closed behind him, sure he had been laughing at her again. Her fingers curled into her palms and she fought the impulse to stamp her foot in sheer frustration. How could Russell have imagined she had anything in common with such an infuriating man?

As she returned to her room and prepared for bed, thoughts of all that had happened in the past week, and especially the past two hours, made her head spin. Expecting to be awake for hours, within moments of her head hitting the pillow she was asleep.

But it was a restless, fitful sleep and waking at six the next morning she was glad to escape the vivid dreams that had filled her mind with images of Nicholas Calder.

But the man in her dreams had borne little resemblance to the arrogant, cynical reality. In her dreams he had been gentle, tender; leaning over her and smiling as he whispered soft words of love. She had looked into his eyes, so close to hers, and been mesmerised. They were dark pools, as deep as oceans. She had wanted to drown in them.

'Stupid idiot. You're being ridiculous,' Maren muttered angrily as she pushed back the sheet and swung her long legs out of bed. 'You're not some lovesick adolescent, you're a grown woman. Pull yourself together. You've worked with men since university. This is no different.'

She stared at her reflection in the mirror. Her face was still flushed from sleep and her hair a wild tangle. There was no mask of cosmetics and elegant hairstyle behind which to hide. She was naked and vulnerable and she saw the truth for the first time.

The men she worked with, had chosen as friends, though outwardly widely different, all had something common. Every one of them had problems of one sort or another. Her relationships with all of them were, despite the occasional tentative skirmish rebuffed and quickly forgotten, friendly rather than romantic.

None had ever challenged her femininity. None had made her fully aware of herself as a woman. Until now. Until him.

'To hell with Nicholas Calder,' Maren hissed at her reflection and spun away from the mirror.

Seven twenty-five found her in the lobby clad in a pale-blue shirt, its long sleeves rolled up past her elbows, and blue cotton trousers. Though her feet were comfortable in the thick, rubber-soled boots she used for fell walking on her visits to her aunt in the Yorkshire Dales, it did seem odd to be wearing them in the tropics.

She had breakfasted on fresh fruit and hot rolls, followed by two cups of coffee. Her suitcase, containing the remainder of her personal belongings, was locked and stored in the manager's office awaiting her return, and her rucksack lay propped against the wall by her feet.

Her gaze strayed once more to the butter-yellow dress in the artifact shop. Would it suit her?

The door opened and Nicholas strode in. As he saw her he seemed surprised. But it was so fleeting she could have imagined it. She knew that in her simple shirt and trousers, her face bare of make-up and her hair drawn back into a ponytail, she looked different, younger, than the previous evening. But she was still the same person.

At the sight of the tall, powerfully-built man who had so disturbed her rest, Maren's heart gave a sudden, extra beat and she quickly bent down to check the fastening on her rucksack so that he would not see the sudden colour in her cheeks.

'Ready?' His tone was abrupt. She was suddenly overwhelmed by apprehension, an awareness that once she stepped outside the hotel with Nicholas Calder she was venturing into unknown territory far more dangerous the tropical forest.

She took a deep breath to steady her quivering nerves. She had come a long way to do this trip. There was no other way to obtain the material she needed to continue her research. She shoved the warning voices to the back of her mind. They were simply the results of jet lag, a restless night, and a perfectly natural reaction to a new experience.

She glanced up. He was watching her, a cynical smile playing at the corners of his mouth, almost as if he could read her thoughts and was waiting for her decision.

She straightened, and swung the rucksack over one shoulder. 'Ready,' she confirmed and walked past him to the door.

'I'll take that.' He put out his hand for her rucksack.

'I can manage,' she said quickly, avoiding his grasp. 'Let's start as we mean to go on, Dr Calder. I don't need allowances made for me. I'll pull my weight.'

His eyes gleamed. 'I'll remember that.' His voice, soft and silky, trickled like ice-water down her spine.

At the end of the path where the hotel garden adjoined the road, a white Land Rover with a large red cross painted on its side was waiting.

Nicholas motioned her to get in. As she slid along the seat and he climbed in after her, the bronzed man behind the wheel stared at Maren in wide-eyed amazement.

'Well, hello there,' he breathed, his blue eyes flicking over her in undisguised admiration.

'This is Dave Edridge, Surgical Registrar at

Goroka Hospital,' Nicholas said briefly, resting his arm along the open window. 'Dave, meet Dr Maren Harvey. She's –' Before he could complete the introduction Dave had seized Maren's right hand in both of his and was pumping it mercilessly.

'Lady, are you a sight for sore eyes,' he whooped in a broad Australian twang, grinning widely. 'Have you come to join our happy band? What's your speciality? Nobody told me you were coming. Nick, you swine, you never let on.'

Maren felt her face grow hot at the Australian's ebullient greeting. Yet it was oddly comforting. His extrovert cheerfulness reminded her of a St Bernard puppy. It was certainly a world away from the welcome she had received from Nicholas.

Maren retrieved her hand with some difficulty. 'Happy to meet you, Dave,' she smiled. 'In order the answers are, no I'm not joining the staff, I'm doing research into resistance to antimalarial drugs, and Dr Calder did not know of my arrival until Professor Brent informed him yesterday.'

'Well, how about that,' the Australian sighed. 'So if you aren't joining the hospital, where are you going?' There was lively curiosity on his pleasant face.

Maren's glance flickered as she was suddenly acutely aware of Nicholas so close behind her. 'Into the Highlands,' she said simply, and watched Dave's sandy eyebrows climb to meet the blond hair that sprang in wiry curls all over his head.

'You mean you –' He switched his gaze to Nicholas. 'Well, how about that? Never again, you said. You swore after –' Dave broke off suddenly and swivelled round on the seat, fumbling for the ignition switch. 'I guess you both want the airstrip, then.' Without waiting for a reply, he put the engine in gear and the Land Rover roared away from the hotel.

Thrown by Dave's abrupt change of subject and curious to know what Nick had sworn not to do and why, Maren settled back on the seat between the two men, casting a sidelong glance at Nicholas. But he was staring straight ahead. His brooding eyes and granite-hewn profile deterred her from asking any questions.

The rain had stopped and the morning sun was already burning the heavy mist from the valley and shrouded mountains. Maren noticed that several of the mountainsides appeared to be free of trees and were instead patched with strips and squares of lighter green.

Keen to learn all she could about this fascinating tropical island, she glanced at Nicholas. But he was lost in his own thoughts which, judging by his expression, were not particularly pleasant.

She turned to Dave. 'What are those lighter patches?'

He followed her pointing finger. 'Kunai grass. The natives here use the slash and burn method of clearing the forest to make their gardens. The majority of the people in this country exist by subsistence farming.' Dave grinned at her. 'It's a pretty good life, really. Plenty of sun, plenty of rain, and good soil that grows just about anything. They make their gardens and grow their crops. Then when the soil is tired, they abandon them and hack out new ones. Sometimes the forest grows back. But often kunai grass takes over instead.'

Maren gazed out on to the lush, exotic greenery, inhaled the rich smell of wet earth and the heady perfume of the tropical flowers.

Dave glanced at her, his sunburned forehead puckered in concern. 'Look, no offence, but do you have any idea what you'll be facing out there?' His wave indicated the thickly forested slopes that rose on either side of the valley, stretching range upon range into the distance.

Maren nodded. 'I think so,' she replied lightly. 'I didn't come expecting it to be a picnic.' She hadn't realised it was going to be quite so difficult either. It would have been so different if she had been going with Russell instead of the tall, silent man beside her.

'When I was young, I imagined the Garden of Eden looked something like this,' she said softly.

Dave's face crumpled into a lopsided grin. 'Yeah, but as well as the proverbial serpent, of which there are several poisonous species, PNG is also blessed with ants, spiders, millipedes ten inches long, and crocodiles.'

Despite the warmth of the climbing sun Maren shivered. *The dark side of paradise.*

'It's no good,' Dave announced above the roar of the engine, his pliable features moulding themselves into an expression of heroic determination. 'I cannot allow you to sacrifice yourself for medical science. Let me take you back to the hospital –' he shot her a pleading look '– I really do need another pair of hands in surgery, especially such pretty ones.'

Maren suppressed a smile. 'I'll take my chances with the ants and the crocodiles.'

Dave shook his head, 'That's what they all say,' he mourned.

Maren laughed and Dave swerved the Land Rover to avoid a group of natives hauling a home-made cart loaded with fruit and vegetables. The violent movement threw Maren against Nicholas and the sudden pressure of his broad shoulders and hard-muscled thigh zinged through her like an electric shock.

She recovered instantly and pulled away, denying her awareness of his body heat through the thin cotton shirt, and the fresh tang of the soap he had used that morning.

Nicholas's dark head came round, his face enigmatic, his eyes unreadable. Maren felt hot colour flood her cheeks and she turned quickly away.

'Are you really short of staff?' she asked Dave. 'Professor Brent told me that the hospital was attached to the medical faculty of the university. Don't you recruit new doctors from there?'

Dave shrugged. 'Nick knows more about that than I do.' He raised his voice over the engine's roar. 'Tell the lady, Nick. Why do we have to import new staff?'

Wishing now that she'd never asked the question, Maren was forced to turn towards Nicholas. But she used the opportunity to change her position and edge away. A deepening of the cynical creases at his mouth told her the movement was not lost on him. She pretended not to notice.

'There are about 300 doctors in the whole of PNG,' Nicholas began, his deep voice clear above the racket. 'But only 60 of those are nationals.'

'Where do all the rest come from, then?' Maren

asked, her interest growing.

Nicholas shrugged. 'The United States, Britain and other European Countries –'

'Don't forget Australia,' Dave put in.

'Who could?' Nicholas retorted. 'And Australia.'

'But why so few from here?' Maren asked, puzzled. 'This is their country. They've got excellent training facilities. Why do they need to rely so heavily on ex-pat medical staff?'

Nicholas's face hardened. 'Graduates from other faculties are generally employed by the government and rise rapidly to positions of influence and financial security. But for medical graduates the rise to power is much slower and the financial rewards correspondingly less. The result is that many of the local doctors are going into private medicine as soon as they can. It all boils down to one thing, Dr Harvey.' His gaze held hers and his mouth twisted. 'Money.' There was no mistaking his contempt.

'I see. Thank you.' She turned away to stare through the windscreen.

A few moments later they arrived at the airstrip. A group of small buildings she guessed were offices stood at one side of the paved turning area. Along from them were several large warehouses. Two lorries were parked beside a twin-engine aircraft that waited, propellers spinning, at the near end of the runway.

Though the airfield was small it had a bustling, businesslike air about it.

'Papers?' Nicholas held out his hand and Maren quickly pulled the plastic wallet containing passes from the various government departments from her trouser pocket.

'Wait here, I won't be long,' Nicholas instructed her and strode off towards the office.

Maren turned to Dave. 'Thanks for the lift.' She offered her hand. 'It was nice meeting you. Are you going straight back to the hospital now?'

Dave nodded, 'As soon as I've collected a consignment of drugs due in from Port Moresby.' He cocked his head on one side. 'You sure you won't change your mind?'

Maren shook her head. 'I have to go.' She slid out of the Land Rover dragging her rucksack behind her. 'Thanks again,' she said over her shoulder.

Dave got out on the other side and slammed the door shut. 'Good luck,' he grinned. 'You'll need it.'

'Still trying to frighten me?' she laughed. 'I'm not afraid of snakes.'

'It wasn't the snakes I was thinking of,' Dave retorted. 'There were two other characters in the Garden of Eden, remember?'

Maren blinked as the implication registered. Then with a brief wave she began walking quickly towards the office, her mind whirling. As she reached the door, Nicholas came through it.

'What's the matter?' His tone was brusque. 'I told you to wait by the Land Rover.'

'So you did,' Maren replied sweetly. 'But Dr Edridge has to collect a drugs consignment and I didn't want to delay him. Have you got the tickets?'

Nicholas nodded. 'Come on, our plane's waiting.'

They retraced their steps to the turning area. Having unloaded their cargo onto the aircraft, the lorries were roaring back to the warehouses.

The pilot leaned forward in the cockpit and gave a cheerful wave that Nicholas returned, then they climbed the steps. Before Maren realised what was happening the door was fastened shut, the engine note climbed to a full-powered scream and she felt a shuddering surge as the brakes were released and the aircraft began to hurtle down the runway.

Chapter Three

Once they were airborne, Maren's long-held breath exploded softly in a relieved sigh and she relaxed back in her seat.

'Surely you're not nervous of flying, Dr Harvey?' Nicholas was gazing at her, amusement in his dark eyes echoed in the ironic twist of his mouth.

'No.' Maren shook her head. 'I like flying. It's take-offs and landings that scare me.' She answered truthfully, without thinking, still finding it hard to accept that, contrary to all her fears, the aeroplane had managed to get off the ground.

As Nicholas's smile deepened Maren realised she had shown him another chink in her defences. She was practically inviting his scorn.

She looked away, glancing round the cabin, noting that they were the only two passengers. She waited for a cutting remark. But to her surprise none came.

'What do you know about this country?' His abrupt question startled her. It was clear from his tone that he expected her to know absolutely nothing.

'Oh, I've managed to learn a little,' she said, masking her irritation.

'Such as?'

She took a deep breath. 'Such as, the island was

discovered in the 16th century by Portuguese navigators. European colonisation began in earnest in the 1880s when Germany took over the north coast and Great Britain the south.

'Australia annexed the German half at the beginning of the First World War, and after the Second War administered New Guinea and what was by then called Papua as one territory. The Dutch handed over the western part of the island to Indonesia in 1963, and Papua New Guinea became self-governing in 1973 and gained independence in 1975.'

Nicholas raised one dark brow. 'Someone's done their homework,' he drawled.

Maren ignored his remark. 'It is one of the largest countries in the Pacific with an area of roughly 179,000 square miles of widely varying terrain, from mountain ranges and steep valleys, to swampy plains and active volcanoes. Rivers flowing from the mountains form some of the largest river systems in the world and in some areas are being harnessed to generate hydro-electric power.'

Nicholas inclined his head and she knew she had made her point. But the mocking gleam in his eyes made her feel like a child caught showing off.

Angry with him and with herself, she turned to look out of the window.

'And the people?' he prompted.

'What about them?' she replied coolly, still staring out of the window.

'Surely you must know something about the people?' he goaded her.

She turned back to him. 'Only that there are over

6 million of them, they speak 700 languages. Only 18 per cent live in urban areas, and the main diseases affecting the general population are malaria, leprosy, tuberculosis, pneumonia, diarrhoea and sexually transmitted diseases. In the urban areas access to a westernised diet has resulted in an increase in diabetes and heart disease.'

A flicker of admiration crossed his craggy features. 'You are a constant surprise to me, Dr Harvey,' he murmured.

'Because I've done some background research?' Maren retorted. 'Surely that's a basic requirement for any expedition?'

'Of course it is –' impatience made him testy '– but after the last –' He broke off, shaking his head. But the memory must have lingered for when he turned back to her his expression was bleak and his eyes slate-hard.

Once again curiosity burned in Maren. That was the second time something had nearly been said about his last expedition. First by Dave in the Land Rover on the way to Goroka airfield, and now by Nicholas. What had happened? From the way Dave had suddenly clammed up and changed the subject, and Nicholas's own tight-lipped fury, it must have been something important. But if it *was* important why had Russell not told her? Perhaps he didn't know. But if Dave knew, then surely …? It was on the tip of her tongue to ask. But Nicholas forestalled her.

'Anyway, let's just say that so far you appear reasonably well prepared.'

'And you, Dr Calder, have a gift for dressing an insult as a compliment.'

His eyes narrowed and a nerve jumped at the point of his jaw. For an instant Maren wondered if she had gone too far. Then, to her surprise she saw his lips twitch in a brief grin.

'Touché,' he murmured. Flexing his massive shoulders he eased himself into a more comfortable position. 'About the people,' he began, and Maren was suddenly aware that their relationship had undergone a subtle change.

'The majority live in small villages and hamlets and exist by cultivating food gardens and keeping pigs. For example, here in the Highlands only a few miles from Goroka or Kainantu, life is much the same as it was in Stone Age Britain.'

'Surely the explorers and occupying countries must have had some effect on the people?' Maren was finding it hard to believe that despite modern technology and methods of travel, there were still people in the world barely touched by civilisation.

'Very little.' Nicholas shook his black head. 'Don't forget the greater part of the country consists of steep, jungle-covered mountains. The coastal plains are sparsely populated because of malaria. The indigenous people are widely scattered in small groups. Few had even seen a white man before the 1930s when prospectors –' He broke off and Maren gasped in fright as the plane suddenly dropped like a stone, then just as quickly shot upwards again.

Reacting instinctively and completely unaware of what she was doing, Maren grabbed Nicholas's arm, all colour draining from her face.

'Relax, Dr Harvey, we aren't about to crash,' he said calmly.

'Are you s – sure?' Maren stuttered, staring at him.

'I'm quite sure.' His cool matter-of-factness helped her control her panic. 'The pilots on the Highland routes call themselves air jockeys because of the CAT caused by the peaks and valleys.'

'CAT?' Maren repeated, the tightness in her throat making her voice husky.

'Clear air turbulence.'

'Oh. Yes. Of course.' She drew in a shaky breath and moistened her dry lips with the tip of her tongue.

The aircraft droned on, bounced and buffeted by the surging air. But the engine pitch remained steady. The realisation that she was still clinging to Nicholas's bare arm broke over Maren in a cold wave. Though he appeared unconcerned, she was suddenly acutely conscious of the texture of his warm, hair-roughened skin, and the muscles bunched like coiled rope beneath her fingers.

Resisting the impulse to snatch her hand away as awareness tingled in her fingertips, she raised it casually to her forehead, smoothing back a stray tendril that curled softly against her temple.

Nicholas's heavy brows lifted fractionally and Maren knew he had placed his own interpretation on her action.

'You were saying?' She strove to match his coolness, furious at her body's betrayal of her confused emotions. 'About prospectors?'

'Ah, yes.' His brooding gaze rested on her flushed cheeks then slid to her mouth. 'They opened up the route which is now the main road into the Highlands from Lae. They were the first white men the Highland people had ever seen.

'What about missionaries?' Maren asked.

'They came later,' he replied. 'The best of them brought education and healthcare to the regions in which they settled.'

'And the others?' She had caught bitterness in his tone.

'Like many of their kind they tried to destroy more than they could possibly build.'

'In what way?' In spite of her self-consciousness under his scrutiny, Maren found her interest caught and held by what he was telling her. He shifted once more in his seat, moving his cramped legs to a more comfortable position.

Under his piercing gaze she had felt as helpless as a butterfly pinned to a board. Now, as she reminded herself of the importance of her job, how it filled her life and left no room for distractions of any kind, especially not an arrogant cynic like Nicholas Calder who was merely her guide on this trip, she felt her strength returning.

Imperceptibly her back straightened. She was in full control once more, her emotions tightly in check. When he had settled himself and turned to her again, she was able to meet his gaze without any reaction, her features composed and a smile of polite enquiry on her lips.

'This country's culture is embodied in legends, in its art forms and in the traditional way of life.' His face hardened as he went on. 'The more devout, or misguided, depending on your point of view, tried to replace the old ways with whatever creed they themselves followed.' His anger was plain. 'Fortunately they didn't entirely succeed. Though many of the initiation rites and ceremonies have been abandoned, along with cannibalism –' at that Maren suppressed a slight shudder '– quite a few of their religious practices based on magic and intercession of spirits or ancestors have been retained in sing-sings. Of course there's also the cargo cult –' Nicholas broke off suddenly. 'I don't suppose you're remotely interested in any of this,' he said flatly.

'You're wrong,' she said. 'I'm fascinated. What were you saying about the cargo cult?'

A frown drew his heavy brows together momentarily as he eyed her, obviously sceptical. 'It was inspired by occurrences during the Second World War. The islanders are waiting for the return of huge birds which will drop from the skies all the goods they want to possess. They believe that when this happens the Europeans will go from PNG, but will leave their goods behind. This often happened during the war.'

Maren nodded. 'It's quite logical really,' she murmured.

There was a jolt, followed almost immediately by another. As she looked out of the window Maren was amazed to see that they had landed. She had been so absorbed by what Nicholas was telling her, she hadn't known a thing about it.

Her face must have mirrored her thoughts for when she turned back he was grinning, his teeth startlingly white against his deeply tanned skin. He leaned towards her and Maren tensed. 'You see, Dr Harvey?' he growled softly, 'the pilot managed all by himself.'

As the plane lurched over the rough grass and

rolled to a jerky stop, he stood up, careful to keep his head bent to avoid hitting the cabin roof.

Maren decided to ignore his dig as she unfastened her seat belt.

As her feet touched the hard ground, she looked around, screwing up her eyes against the bright sun climbing rapidly in a cloudless sky.

The mountains towered above her, their thickly forested slopes seeming almost vertical and shockingly close in the warm clear air. Glancing the other way she realised for the first time just how short and narrow the valley was.

Her knees were suddenly weak. How had the pilot dared? He must have nerves of steel to take off and land on a strip of rough grass no longer than a football pitch and barely as wide.

Her thoughts were interrupted by Nicholas dumping both rucksacks on the ground beside her. Maren immediately picked hers up and slung it over her shoulders, determined not to give Nicholas Calder the opportunity to make any more scathing remarks about her readiness or suitability for this expedition.

Settling the rucksack more comfortably, she looked up to see Nicholas regarding her with folded arms and a quizzical expression. 'Where do you think you're going?' he enquired, raising one heavy brow.

Maren was taken aback. 'I thought … You said we'd be walking. What does it look as if I'm doing?' she finished in exasperation.

'Your enthusiasm does you credit,' he said drily. 'It also reveals your lack of experience. With the mileage we have to cover and the terrain involved, we don't walk unless there is absolutely no alternative.

Patience, Dr Harvey, you'll be walking soon enough. Then no doubt you'll wish you weren't.' He turned away.

Maren shrugged the rucksack off and dropped it on the ground. Biting her lip to hold back the angry words she longed to fling in his arrogant face she drew a slow deep breath.

She stared thoughtfully at Nicholas's broad back as he raised his arm in salute to a gunmetal-blue Land Rover roaring towards them, followed by two heavy, battered- looking trucks.

Why was she reacting so violently where he was concerned? She had always thought of herself as a calm person. Her upbringing had schooled her to control her feelings. After the disastrous episode with Paul she had turned the key on her emotions. Locked away they could do no damage, freeing her to concentrate on her work.

But since that first meeting with Nicholas Calder less than 24 hours ago, it was as though a jagged rock had splashed into the smooth pond of her life, exploding its glassy stillness, plunging down to unexpected depths. It had sent waves and ripples in ever-widening circles, causing treacherous undercurrents, and stirring up dangerous, shocking dreams, clouding her normally clear mind, leaving her shaken and disorientated.

Nicholas swung round, making her jump. 'This is the last chance to change your mind,' he warned her. 'Once the plane has unloaded it flies back to Goroka. There's no way out after that.'

His dark eyes held hers. His face was expressionless, a hard mask revealing nothing of the

40

thoughts behind it. The decision was hers.

Despite the hot sun, gooseflesh pimpled Maren's bare arms as trepidation trailed icy fingers down her spine. Then, as if from a long way off she heard her own voice. 'I'm going on.'

Nicholas studied her for a moment longer, gave a brief nod, and turned to greet the stocky black man climbing out of the Land Rover. The uniform smartness of his dazzlingly white shirt and shorts was enhanced by a black leather briefcase and two cardboard folders gripped in his left hand.

'Morning, Bilas,' Nicholas shouted above the throaty roar of the two trucks which were slewing round to halt beside the silent plane.

'Good morning, Dr Calder.' A wide grin split his face as they shook hands. 'A pleasure to see you again.'

Maren was aware of a lively curiosity in the deep brown eyes that swivelled from Nicholas to her and back again. Nicholas must seen it too for his tone had an ironic edge as he made the introductions with grave formality. 'Dr Harvey, may I present Bilas Kanawe from the Okapa Administrative Office. Bilas, this is Dr Maren Harvey who is here to gather data on resistance to antimalarial drugs.'

As Maren extended her hand she noticed how strongly the features of the government official resembled those of an Australian aborigine.

'Mr Kanawe,' she murmured politely.

'It is a pleasure to meet you, Dr Harvey,' the dapper little man replied in faultless English with barely a trace of an accent. 'I have here some information which may be of use to you.' He extracted one of the folders and presented it to Maren. 'Statistics on the increase of malaria in this province, increase percentages of the three different types of malaria, mortality and relapse rates, plus antimalarial drugs prescribed.'

'How very kind of you, Mr Kanawe.' Maren was surprised and delighted. She accepted the folder eagerly, unable to resist opening the flap to take a quick look inside.

The little man beamed, his chest visibly expanding beneath the crisp shirt front. 'It is always a privilege to be of assistance to Professor Brent. And of course his esteemed colleagues,' he added quickly, anxious that she was not offended.

Russell was an angel. The figures would certainly save her a lot of time and extra work.

The coughing rumble of the plane's twin engines brought Maren's head up. The trucks, now laden with the crates and boxes from the aircraft were lurching and bumping down the airstrip perimeter as the plane swung round to taxi to the far end ready for take-off.

'It must have cost you considerable time and effort to collect these figures so quickly, Mr Kanawe,' Maren shouted above the noise.

Bilas shook his head vigorously. 'Really it was not difficult. The government is most concerned about this problem and the Health Department has requested all administrative offices to ensure that monthly returns are made, in triplicate, of all patients seen by medical personnel in hospitals, health centres, sub-centres and aid posts in the province, listing diagnosis and treatment, also any other relevant facts.'

Maren caught the inside of her bottom lip between her teeth trying to suppress a smile. Bilas Kanawe was the perfect government employee – earnest, efficient and even talking like a memo.

Nicholas caught her eye, bending his head so she could hear him above the roar. 'Papua New Guinea has recognised what makes a country truly civilised,' he said, his expression serious. 'Mountains of paperwork.' Though his face did not alter, his eyes reflected her own wry amusement.

He turned back to the little man, leaving Maren unnerved by the pleasure that moment of rapport had given her. 'Bilas, have you managed to track down where those kuru reports came from?'

Bilas nodded, earnestness replaced by another beaming smile. 'Indeed I have, doctor. My cousin works in the Gimi Census Division sub-office. He confirmed that two cases of kuru have been reported to the aid post there.'

'Thanks, Bilas –' Nicholas clapped him on the shoulder '– You've been a great help.'

The warmth of Nicholas's smile as he looked down at the little man caused Maren an odd pang. It was the first time she had seen him smile properly. Quickly she looked away, flipping open the file once more and riffling through the neatly-typed pages.

'I am merely doing my job,' Bilas Kanawe said, ducking his head modestly while pride threatened to burst the buttons off his shirt.

A piercing whistle caught their attention and they all turned to see the pilot waving a beckoning arm.

'I see departure is imminent,' Bilas said quickly. 'My best wishes to you both for a safe and productive expedition.' He shook hands with Maren then with Nicholas. 'One word of warning, there is rumour of tribal fighting between some of the Gimi and South Fore people. It is most difficult to obtain confirmation. Possibly hostilities have ceased. But I advise caution.'

Tucking his briefcase more securely under his arm he trotted away, suddenly stopping to call back to them. 'Forgive me, but regulations require that I ask if you are both taking antimalarial tablets.'

Nicholas and Maren both shouted, 'Yes!' Bilas scuttled away down the field, giving them one last wave before disappearing inside the plane and securing the door behind him.

Moments later the aircraft hurtled past them, plastering their clothes to their bodies, the force of the prop-wash whipping Maren's hair across her face. Just as she was convinced it would overshoot the runway and crash into the mountainside directly ahead, it soared skyward in a steep banking climb and disappeared behind a peak.

She stared after it but could no longer hear the engines. The silence made her very much aware that her last link with the outside world had gone. She was alone with Nicholas Calder and the tropical rainforest. Which would be more unfriendly?

Chapter Four

During the next hour neither spoke. Nicholas seemed preoccupied as he drove at what Maren thought was a reckless speed along a rough dirt road hacked out of the mountainside.

The heat was a lead weight, sapping her strength and dulling her mind. The sun blazed fiercely. Though all the windows were wound down, the fine mesh screens which kept mosquitoes and other insects out also prevented the air circulating. The humidity was stifling. Just sitting there she was bathed in a dew of perspiration.

They were climbing steadily. She looked back once and recognised the airstrip. It was terrifyingly small, and the only piece of level ground in the entire valley which snaked out of sight far below. She did not look again.

They passed two junctions where the dirt road divided and curved off down to the left, disappearing almost at once into the virgin rainforest. There were no signposts or markers at these junctions. At the second one Maren could not contain her curiosity.

'Where does it lead?'

'To Okapa,' Nicholas replied. 'It was the site of the first Patrol Post set up in the area by the

Australian Government in 1956.'

'Why did they site it here?' It seemed such a remote and difficult place to reach. There was no denying the beauty of the thickly forested mountains and steep valleys, broken here and there by the curving blue snake of a river, or the white ribbon of a waterfall. But it was a wild, primitive beauty, hostile and dangerous.

'It's a central point from which to cover the whole south-western area of the province.'

'Do any Europeans live there?' Though it was an effort to talk she wanted to learn more about this fascinatingly diverse country.

Nicholas nodded. 'A few missionaries who run their own churches and healthcare centres. There are several white staff in the provincial hospital, some developing coffee and copra as commercial crops, some in the hydro-electric power plant, water-treatment and sewage works, radio stations –'

'They have radio?' Maren was surprised.

He nodded. 'Karai AM and FM broadcasts from Port Moresby in English for the younger audience. Regional stations broadcast from Goroka in Tok Pisin and other languages for older people. It's their only contact with the rest of the country, apart from the delivery of supplies by plane and helicopter,' he explained shortly.

The road was deteriorating. Nicholas had to keep, slowing down to avoid potholes and deep ruts in the rough surface. Sweat beaded his face and darkened the back and underarms of his shirt. Though he had answered her questions he seemed disinclined to chat. Maren retreated into silence.

She was thoroughly uncomfortable. Her clammy shirt and trousers were sticking to her and the chafing constriction of her bra was unbearable. Too late she remembered it was nylon. Now she understood Russell's insistence on absorbent cotton for all clothes.

Pulling out her damp, crumpled handkerchief she wiped her face and neck once again, shifting restlessly. She darted a look at Nicholas, but his attention was focused on the road ahead.

She hated having to ask and wished he would suggest a brief halt. But from the determined pace of his driving, stopping was the last thing on his mind.

'Can you pull over for a moment?' Maren tried to be matter-of-fact but her cheeks grew warm under his frowning glance.

'What on earth for?' he demanded impatiently. 'We've covered barely 15 miles.'

'A very bumpy 15 miles.' She looked at her watch. 'It's over three hours since we left the hotel. I'm not a camel. I need to stop for a moment.'

Nicholas swung the Land Rover to the edge of the track where trees, shrubs and dense undergrowth grew in a seemingly impenetrable wall. He switched off the engine and in the silence Maren heard for the first time the shriek and twitter of birds.

Flexing his shoulders, he rested both arms on the steering wheel and glared at her. 'Don't go more than three feet off the track and don't be long,' he warned her.

Maren gritted her teeth. She opened the door and as she turned to climb out her shirt made a soft tearing sound as it peeled away from the seat.

Perspiration broke out afresh as she slammed the door and walked round the front of the vehicle, screwing up her eyes against the sun's brightness, conscious of Nicholas watching her through the windscreen.

The air was still and moist, heavy with the foetid smell of damp earth and rotting vegetation. Insects buzzed and whined. She quickly rolled her sleeves down. Although sunset was the worst time for mosquitoes there was no point in taking chances.

Cautiously she pushed aside the tangled ropes of vines and lianas. Leaves rustled and danced as tiny creatures skittered away, frightened by this rare intrusion.

She had taken only a few steps off the track, but glancing over her shoulder she could no longer see the break in the trees, nor the comfortingly solid shape of the Land Rover. The forest had closed around her, enfolding her in its oppressive green gloom. She swallowed her momentary panic. She had wanted privacy and she had certainly got it.

Slipping out of her shirt she quickly unhooked her bra and tossed it over the curving frond of a huge fern. As she rebuttoned her shirt her awareness of her body, naked beneath the damp cotton, surprised her, and the delicious sensation of freedom made her feel slightly guilty.

She was about to return to the Land Rover when it occurred to her that she had better make full use of the discreet screen of the forest. Nicholas Calder would certainly not take kindly to another stop within the next three hours.

A few moments later, as she turned towards the

track, she unwittingly trod on a tonguelike fungus growing out of a decaying tree. Her foot slid from under her and, unable to save herself, she crashed down onto the forest floor, her breath driven from her body in a grunting cry as she landed on her back in the thick humus of rotting leaves. Her other foot kicked part of the dead wood away and immediately a flood of termites poured over her boot.

A lizard darted over the tree in a flash of green and silver, disappearing again almost at once. Two giant millipedes, the colour of dried blood, their legs a rippling fringe on each side of their flattened bodies, squirmed out of sight beneath the dirty-yellow fungoid growth which gave off a sickly sweet smell where Maren's boot had crushed it.

Above her, startled by the noise, black cockatoos screeched harshly, their cheeks of bare skin flushed brilliant crimson with alarm. Gasping, Maren scrambled to her feet, kicking out wildly to rid herself of the termites. She crashed through the undergrowth, heedless of the creepers that hung in tangled skeins, binding trees together, a living net to trap the unwary.

Heart thudding, hair disordered and matted with bits of leaf and twig, she burst free of the forest's clutching fingers and found herself back on the track, the Land Rover barely a couple of yards away.

Trembling with shock and relief, Maren gulped in great breaths of hot, humid air as she brushed dirt and leaves off her trousers. Thank heavens she'd had them tucked into her socks and boots, otherwise the termites – She shut off the thought with an inward shudder. Tugging the band from her hair she shook it free of debris then gathered it once again into a ponytail.

By the time she opened the door and climbed into the Land Rover, even though she was sweating freely, she had recovered her poise.

Nicholas stared at her, a frown drawing his heavy brows together. 'What happened?'

She shrugged lightly. 'I slipped.'

'Are you hurt?' He sounded more irritated than sympathetic. But as she shook her head, he reached forward and without a word carefully extricated a piece of dead leaf from the "v" of her shirt.

Maren's face flamed at the intimacy of the gesture and, highly conscious that she now wore nothing beneath the thin cotton, she raised the hand nearest him to her neck in a protective, warding-off movement.

He merely smiled and started the engine and they resumed their jolting progress along the track.

It was only then that Maren realised. In her panic to get back to the Land Rover after her fall, she had left her bra hanging on the giant fern. She turned to Nicholas, caught herself in time and turned back, unable to hide a smile at the mental picture of some future explorer finding it, and postulating theories as to how a flimsy scrap of white lace and nylon came to be dangling in the tropical rainforest halfway up a mountain in New Guinea.

'Care to share the joke?'

The man had eyes like a hawk. Maren shook her head quickly. 'It was nothing.' Then, because she could see he didn't believe her and was ready to pursue the matter, which she definitely wasn't, she twisted round on the seat.

'What are you doing?' Nicholas demanded, not taking his eyes from the rutted road.

'I'm thirsty. I've got a bottle of Perrier water in –'

'Perrier?' He shot her a brief glance. Then his mouth curled. 'It figures.' His voice hardened. 'Save it.' It was an order. 'I don't know how long it will take us to reach the first village. It depends on the state of the road. If you must have a drink, there's a flask of iced fruit juice in the left-hand pocket of my pack.'

Just for an instant Maren was tempted to tell him what he could do with his flask. But she dismissed the impulse even as it occurred, already anticipating the blissful sensation of ice-cool liquid in her parched mouth.

She knelt on the seat, bracing herself with her knees against the jolting motion of the vehicle, while she reached over and extricated the flask.

'Perhaps it will improve,' she suggested, swivelling round again, clutching the flask against her as the Land Rover lurched and swayed, bumping her against the door. 'When do we reach the main road?'

'This is the main road,' he retorted with heavy patience. 'It's the only road to where we're going. What did you expect, motorways?' He glared at her briefly. 'I warned you this was going to be a rough trip.'

'I'm not complaining,' Maren flashed back. 'Not about the conditions anyway.'

Nicholas slammed on the brakes and the Land Rover jerked to a halt.

Maren swallowed as he twisted deliberately round to face her, sliding one arm along the back of the seat.

'All right, what *are* you complaining about?' His reasonable tone did not fool her for a moment. But in her anger she ignored the warning signs.

'You,' she blurted out. 'Your attitude. I had to pass some stupid test of your own devising before you'd even agree to bring me on this trip. Since then you've consistently belittled me. And for some reason best known to yourself, you seem intent on making me feel about as welcome as the plague.'

'Why would I want to do that?'

I don't know. You tell me.'

Nicholas leaned forward, 'How did you want to be welcomed?' His eyes bored into hers. 'What exactly did you expect, hmm?' His deep voice was soft and mesmeric and Maren didn't realise he had moved until his right hand was cupping her chin, his thumb tilting it up. But by then it was too late.

'Was this what you were waiting for?' he growled, shutting out the light, filling her vision.

She froze then dropped the flask as she jerked backwards, her hands coming up. But he anticipated the move. In an instant his arm was around her, pressing her against him, crushing her breasts against the solid wall of his chest.

'No.' Her fear-filled cry died as it was born, silenced abruptly as his mouth came down on hers in a savage, punishing kiss that bruised her lips against her teeth, forcing them apart. His hot exploring tongue shocked her to the very depths of her being.

Maren strained backwards, pushing against his shoulders, fear and fury lending her strength. But the only effect of her desperate struggles was an inexorable tightening of his vicelike grip. Then, to her shame and horror, a different sensation lanced through her. A shaft of melting sweetness, so exquisite it was agony.

The shattering impact of her body's betrayal was like a physical blow. She went limp in his arms.

At that moment, as if sensing the change in her, Nicholas tore his mouth from hers, releasing her so suddenly that she swayed towards him before realising she was free. Without a word he turned away, his face as cold and hard as granite as he restarted the engine.

Heart pounding, Maren leaned down and picked up the flask. By some miracle it hadn't broken.

As she tried to unscrew the top, pretending normality in a world that would never be normal again, her fingers trembled uncontrollably. She kept her face averted, gazing blindly out of the side window, her eyes opened very wide so that the scalding tears would not fall.

She did not know why she felt like weeping. He was utterly contemptible. How dare he assume she had wanted … He had forced her, taken advantage of his superior strength.

Suddenly, shockingly, she was reliving the pressure of his mouth on hers, the ache in her breasts as her body had been crushed against his, and she had to acknowledge the truth. If that kiss had lasted a second longer, she would have responded.

Never before had she been kissed with such deliberate and cynical expertise, nor experienced that gut-wrenching, breathtaking stab of desire. What was happening to her? Was she mad? Had she not learned from bitter experience that involvement with a man meant pain and humiliation?

But a small voice deep inside reminded her that the affair with Paul had ended years ago. And it was a long time since she had felt a man's arms around her, such a long, long time.

Damn Nicholas Calder. She had been perfectly happy, her life tidy and uncomplicated. Now in the space of a few seconds, emotions she had long thought safely buried had suddenly erupted, threatening her calm orderly existence. She hated him for that. He had no regard for her as a person. On the slenderest evidence he had formed an opinion, and despite her attempts to correct it, that brutal travesty of a kiss had been merely to prove his point.

Well, if that was how he saw her that was how she would be. She could more easily bear his contempt for the woman he thought she was, than admit the doubts, fears, and loneliness she had managed so long to deny. Let him think what he liked. Why should she care? She was here to do medical research. She knew her job, and nothing could shake her belief in herself as far as that was concerned.

And as a woman? She shoved that thought away. But it lingered, hovering on the edge of her consciousness. To escape its taunting echo, she slid into her sophisticated shell. She would act out the role he had chosen for her.

'Are you all right?' he demanded tersely, concentrating on the track ahead.

'Of course,' she was able to reply with exactly the right amount of surprise. 'Why wouldn't I be?'

He darted her a look, as if he had expected a different answer. Then his mouth curled. 'Of course,' he repeated with quiet irony. 'Why wouldn't you be?'

Maren wasn't prepared for the sudden chill that gripped her heart. But she had made her decision. There was no turning back.

She managed to get the top off the flask, and carefully poured out half a cup of juice. As it trickled down her throat, deliciously cool and refreshing, she leaned back against the seat and closed her eyes.

How could Russell have done this to her? How could he ever have imagined that she and Nicholas Calder had anything in common except their profession? He must be getting old. She had never imagined that happening to him. But there was no doubt about it, his judgment, once so sharp, so accurate, had failed him.

Maren savoured the last drops from the cup. The mixture of lemon and pineapple had been tangy but smooth, and so welcome. She started to replace the cap then took it off and half-filled it once more.

'Here you are, Nick,' she said brightly. 'I dare say you're thirsty too.'

He arched one dark brow at her then took the cup, tossing the contents back in two swallows.

'Nick is for my friends,' he said without expression as he handed back the cup. 'You can call me Nicholas.'

'What about your family?' Maren was surprised that the rebuff stung. After all, what did it matter? She was no friend of his and never would be. 'What do they call you?'

'I have no family,' he replied coldly. 'Now do you mind if we drop the subject?'

'Not at all. No ties, no troubles, isn't that what

they say?'

He did not reply. Maren cringed. How brittle and shallow she sounded. It was all going wrong. She racked her brain to find a safe subject for conversation. Silence would allow her thoughts to run wild and she wasn't ready for that. Medicine was their only common interest and that reminded her of something.

'What is the "kuru" you and Mr Kanawe were talking about? I haven't heard the word before. Is it a disease?'

Nicholas eyed her briefly then nodded. 'It means shivering or trembling in the Fore language. It's a disease of the central nervous system, and unique as it only affects this one particular tribal group.'

'What, nobody else in the entire world?'

'No, not that particular strain.'

'That's incredible.' Maren's interest was immediate and total. 'Is it infectious or contagious? How is it transmitted?'

Nicholas seemed mildly amused by her interest. 'We're as certain as we can be that it was caused by a virus, but unlike any previously known.'

'You said "was". What do you mean? How is it passed on now?'

'It isn't,' Nicholas replied. 'Kuru has been dying out since the late 1960s when the method of transmission was discovered and halted.'

'So how was it transmitted?' Maren was absorbed in the discussion. The tension around her eyes and mouth was smoothed away as all other thoughts were pushed aside.

'By ritual cannibalism,' Nicholas answered

56

calmly.

'Oh.' Maren was slightly shaken. It was one thing hearing or reading about such matters in a modern city on the other side of the world, but it was rather different being in the place where it actually happened. 'But the Fore people aren't headhunters in the usual sense, are they?' she couldn't help a little tingle of apprehension.

Nicholas shook his head impatiently. 'In general they are a gentle, hospitable people, particularly towards Europeans. The consumption of human flesh was a mourning rite, and restricted to close relatives. It was also a mark of love and respect, a wish to remain close to the dead person and to preserve their good qualities inside themselves.'

'If the agent causing the disease was a virus –' Maren rubbed her forehead as she tried to fit the pieces together '– why wasn't it killed when the meat was cooked?'

'For two reasons,' Nicholas replied. 'Firstly, this virus is unique. It cannot be destroyed by heat, formaldehyde or radiation. Secondly, ritual cannibalism only takes place at a mourning feast. At feasts meat and vegetables are wrapped in leaves or stuffed into bamboo cylinders and cooked in steam pits instead of over the usual open fire. But because the Fore people live quite high up in the mountains, between 4,000 and 7,000 feet above sea level, the boiling point of water is lower. Also it's men who are in charge of the steam pit. They decide the cooking time, which can be very erratic. So the meat is rarely cooked right through.'

'Does the virus live in any particular part of the

body?' Maren wiped her face and neck again. It was going to take longer than she thought to adjust to the sticky heat.

'It has been found in all parts, but the highest concentration is in the brain.' Nicholas swung the wheel hard over to avoid a deep fissure in the track, throwing Maren against the door.

She gasped as the wing nuts holding the mesh screen over the open window dug in just below her shoulder.

'Sorry about that,' Nicholas muttered as he wrenched the wheel back again. 'Are you all right?'

'Fine,' she grimaced, rubbing her sore arm. She would have two lovely purple bruises by evening. They'd match the ones on her bottom from all the jolting.

'I'd better take a look.' Nicholas changed down a gear and swung the Land Rover over to the side of the track. 'In this climate even a simple scratch can lead to a tropical ulcer.'

'No, don't stop,' Maren said quickly. 'There's no need. I'm quite all right. The skin isn't broken. It was only a bump.' He must not stop. He must not touch her. The memory of that kiss was all too vivid. 'Does kuru affect men and women equally?'

Nicholas revved the engine and kept the vehicle moving up the track. He shot her a mocking glance. 'Are you by any chance trying to impress me?'

'You flatter yourself,' Maren retorted with a coolness she certainly didn't feel. 'I see no point in prolonging this journey with unnecessary stops.' He opened his mouth, but she hurried on before he could speak. 'I told you, the disease is new to me. Naturally

58

I'm interested.'

'Oh, naturally,' he agreed with heavy irony. Maren fought the overwhelming urge to hit him.

'Look, I'd like to know more about kuru. But if you don't want to talk just say so. After all, you are driving and it must be terribly difficult to do both at the same time.'

'Careful,' he growled, his eyes gleaming dangerously. A derisive smile lifted the corners of his mouth. 'Such single-mindedness and dedication. What an example for my students.' His expression did not change but his voice hardened. 'What a pity you lack their courtesy.'

Maren flushed. She had deserved that. She could not understand herself. Good manners were normally instinctive to her. It was him. He was enough to try the patience of a saint.

'In my view, respect has to be earned,' she countered stubbornly.

'By everyone except you, it seems.' He had neatly trapped her.

She glanced sideways, unexpectedly catching his eye. He raised one dark brow in sardonic challenge and she quickly turned her head away, staring out of the side window. All right, maybe he had a point, but he didn't have to be so infuriatingly smug.

'Among the Fore people kuru is regarded as a women's disease,' he said. 'Affected women outnumber men by roughly two to one.'

'Why is that?' Maren was vastly relieved that the conversation had returned to medicine.

'The main reason is that men had less to do with dismembering the body and preparing it for cooking.

Though the older men sometimes took part in the feast, especially if the kinship was a close one, they rarely ate women relatives or kuru victims. Warriors also abstained through fear that cannibalism would diminish their fighting prowess.'

'In that case it seems strange that men were affected at all,' Maren pondered.

'That's a good point.' The careless compliment pleased her more than she liked to admit. 'Something else that makes the disease unique is the length of time between infection by the virus and development of the disease. Kuru is the first chronic or sub-acute degenerative disease which has proved to be a slow virus infection.'

Maren's brain was racing. 'Do you mean that if a boy ate human flesh contaminated with the kuru virus when he was a child, but did not touch it ever again, he could still develop the disease 15 or 20 years later?'

Nicholas nodded grimly. 'On average, incubation is 14 years. But latency in genetically resilient cases has been 40 years. It's a time bomb, ticking quietly away in the brain until something, we still don't know what, triggers it. Then –' he hit the steering wheel with the flat of his hand making Maren jump '– another victim.'

'How long –' she began.

'From onset to death? About a year.'

Something was puzzling Maren. 'I thought you said that kuru only occurred among the Fore people.'

'I did,' Nicholas replied.

'But you asked Mr Kanawe about two cases reported in the Gimi area.'

'That is because there are other central nervous system disturbances with symptoms that resemble kuru occurring in the Highlands. However up to now we've found that reports of kuru outside the Fore boundaries are either one of these other diseases, or can be traced directly to Fore ancestry.'

'What a fascinating study,' Maren murmured, mentally listing the research procedures she would employ if she were investigating the disease. She was shocked and bewildered by the expression of intense dislike that darkened Nicholas's face as he glanced at her.

'These aren't inanimate objects we're discussing,' he grated, 'they are people.'

'I didn't mean –' Maren began, but he cut across her.

'Save it,' he said tersely.

Maren clenched her teeth. The man was absolutely impossible. She had not meant to sound callous. She had been trained not to allow personal feelings to influence her approach to her work. He was being totally unfair. He'd have been the first to complain if she had reacted with horror when he'd mentioned cannibalism. He would have criticised her lack of objectivity.

She flexed her shoulders and arched her back, easing the stiffness and freeing her shirt where perspiration had glued it to the seat. How much longer would she have to endure the Land Rover's lurching and jolting? How much further did Nicholas expect to travel today? She was hot, tired and grubby. What wouldn't she give for a cool shower, or even the chance to get out and stretch her legs.

She could imagine his reaction if she asked. His mouth would curl into that contemptuous smile she had come to loathe, and he would remind her of her claim to be perfectly able to cope with the conditions. Well, she would show him. No way was Nicholas Calder going to have the satisfaction of saying, "I told you so!"

'I don't know about you, but I'm hungry,' he said suddenly.

So he did have some human needs after all. Maren glanced at her watch. Almost one. It would be wonderful to get out of this bone-shaking tin oven and feel sound ground beneath her feet again.

'The hotel packed some food for me: bread, cold meat and fruit. We can share it,' she offered, ready to overlook his antagonism in her relief at the prospect of a break in their journey. She knelt round on the seat, leaning over to reach her rucksack.

'Fine,' he agreed, 'we can have what I brought later.'

Maren pulled out the foil-wrapped packages and bumped down on the seat again. She glanced expectantly at him. He took his eyes from the track just long enough to note the food on her lap.

'Are we going to eat, or do you want to sit and hold it?'

Maren struggled to hide her disappointment. 'We're not stopping then?'

Nicholas shook his head. 'As you so rightly said, there's no point in prolonging this journey with unnecessary stops.'

Compressing her lips, Maren began opening the packages. She folded slices of succulent ham into fresh, crusty rolls, handed one to Nicholas and bit into the other.

They ate in silence, finishing their picnic with bananas and slices of mango which, though delicious and refreshing, left Maren feeling more sticky than ever.

They were now high in the mountains. As the Land Rover climbed yet another ridge and rounded yet one more bend, Maren was able to look across over the thickly covered hillsides to more mountains beyond.

Clouds were once more beginning to appear over the farthest peaks warning of rain that would fall later. She scanned the slopes and ridges. 'How long before we reach a village?' she asked, searching for some sign of human habitation.

'We've passed several already,' Nicholas told her.

'But I didn't see anything.'

'You don't know what to look for,' he replied bluntly. 'Out here away from the influence of European settlements, the Fore people live in villages quite different from those we know. Their hamlets may consist of only two or three widely separated houses, with food gardens or secondary forest growth between them.'

Nicholas shook his head. 'Missionaries and administration have tried, and in some cases succeeded, in reorganising hamlets into larger and more compact nuclear-style family units.' There was anger in his voice warning Maren that this was a touchy subject. 'However, in many cases, the people have drifted back to the traditional lifestyle where women and girls share one or two houses with their babies, while the married men and uninitiated boys have a house of their own, usually near the edge of the forest.'

'You believe that's a better way of living?' Maren asked sceptically.

'It has a lot to recommend it,' Nicholas's reply was deceptively mild.

'I suppose that's because you don't believe in marriage and family life.'

'Why should you suppose that?' His coolly appraising glance unsettled Maren. 'My personal preferences have nothing to do with it. The Fore have very strong family ties. All age groups have a part to play in society. The old are respected for their wisdom and skills, which they pass on to the young who are keen to learn. The marriage bond is sacred and adultery is disapproved of and punished. Children are freely exchanged and adopted by relatives and friends. Even in warfare the captured women and children are integrated into the winning side and only the men killed. The sick and wounded are looked after by the community.' He smiled grimly. 'How uncivilised they are, compared to us.'

Maren stared out of the window. What a complex man he was. Just as she had decided he was the most cynical, hard-hearted, arrogant man she had ever met, he revealed a deep and passionate concern for the native people of this country. Yet to her, a fellow doctor and as English as himself, he was almost hostile. Why?

'But things can't just be left as they've always been,' she said at last. 'There has to be progress.'

'I'm not against progress, if it really is progress,'

Nicholas allowed. 'But I'm dead against change for change's sake. Haven't you ever noticed how the underdeveloped countries are infested with so-called experts declaring, "We want to help you, so you must abandon all your old beliefs and traditions and do as we tell you".' He shook his head. 'It's such bloody arrogance.'

Maren was rather shaken to find she agreed with him. She hadn't looked at it that way before.

'Perhaps their methods are sometimes a bit clumsy,' she admitted. 'But the intentions are good. For example, missionaries are usually the first people to bring any kind of medical care to primitive countries. Without them people would still be dying from endemic diseases like leprosy, TB and malaria.'

'True,' Nicholas said flatly, 'the missionaries bring medicines and they don't ask for money. No, they only demand the souls of those they help. So in order to please these newcomers and ensure the supply of medicines and anything else new and therefore intriguing, a culture spanning hundreds of years is abandoned in less than a generation. Then after the missionaries, commercial prospectors, oil drillers, copper and gold miners and trade store owners arrive. So instead of dying from leprosy, TB and malaria, the natives can now choose measles, gastroenteritis, influenza and STDs as alternatives.'

Despite the heat, Maren shivered under his fierce anger.

'And you,' he grated, as she opened her mouth, 'God alone knows what damage you've done.'

Chapter Five

'*Me*?' Maren jerked round in her seat, startled by his bitter accusation. 'What are you talking about?'

'The growing resistance to antimalarials.' He hurled the words at her like missiles. 'It could be one of the gravest situations this country has ever faced.'

'You're holding *me* responsible?'

'Don't be facetious,' he snapped. 'You know damn well I mean all those like you, involved in developing newer and stronger drugs.' He ran impatient fingers through his thick black hair. 'Hell, isn't it obvious that far from wiping out disease you're actively encouraging more virulent organisms? Look at what happened with penicillin and other antibiotics.' He snorted in disgust. 'History just goes on repeating itself. People go on dying and the pharmaceutical companies make fortunes and perpetuate the cycle.'

'Now hang on just a minute!' Maren was seething. 'I am not, nor have I ever been involved in commercial drug development.' Her face and throat burned with indignation. 'I happen to be totally opposed to the indiscriminate use of drugs, for all the reasons you so clearly defined.'

'But your work is aimed at producing yet another –'

'A vaccine,' Maren interrupted. 'There is a difference.'

'Is that so?' Nicholas's sarcasm was biting, 'Yet you're still treating effects not causes.'

'Of course we are,' Maren shouted at him. 'Because we don't have any choice.' She took a deep breath, making a determined effort to control her temper. 'Listen, the malaria germ is carried by pregnant female mosquitoes: the males are harmless.' *Unlike the human variety.* Her fleeting thought was accompanied by a vivid memory of the fear that had frozen her to immobility the instant before his mouth had ravaged hers. The break in her concentration lasted only a split-second, but it threw her off balance.

'Th – there are three ways to kill them,' she stammered. 'By spraying oil on the still water where they breed to prevent the newly hatched larvae from breathing.' Her voice grew stronger, her confidence returned. 'By putting special fish in the water to eat the larvae. Or by spraying the adults with insecticide.' She spread her hands, smiling sweetly. 'Simple, isn't it?'

She paused. 'But there is just one small problem. As the breeding grounds are in tropical swamps and jungles, covering hundreds of square miles, unapproachable on foot and invisible from the air, it's impossible to get the oil sprays, the fish and the insecticide to where they are needed.' Despite her determination to stay calm, Maren was finding it very hard. 'So, as we can't treat the cause, we follow the only course left open and treat the effects. Why a vaccine? Because one injection giving permanent immunity is obviously preferable to long-term drug prevention or treatment.'

She sat back and wiped her face and neck once more, pulling her shirt free of her clammy skin.

'No wonder you're hot,' Nicholas observed dryly. 'All that fire and fury. You're hardly the dispassionate scientist.'

Maren glared at him. 'That's rich, coming from you! In any case I think I've been remarkably dispassionate, all things considered. Do you imagine you're the first person to point out we're treating effects not causes?'

His slight smile seemed to mock her and Maren's irritation exploded into real anger.

'Can't you see it's only a matter of time before resistance becomes so widespread we'll be relying on combinations of quinine and tetracycline as a last resort, regardless of the appalling risks?'

Nicholas sighed, shaking his black head. 'You'd be far more effective without the dramatics.'

Maren faced him, knowing and not caring that dislike was vivid on her face. 'You're despicable,' she said quietly. 'It's perfectly all right for you to get angry or excited about the things you believe in. But if I do it, I'm melodramatic. You deliberately taunt me then adopt this patronising, holier-than-thou attitude whenever I defend myself.'

The moment the words were out, she knew she'd made a mistake.

'Defend yourself?' he echoed. 'Does asking questions about your work constitute an attack on you, then?'

'Yes – no ...' Once again he had her hopelessly

confused. 'It's the way you – you weren't just asking questions, you were forcing me to justify what I do.'

He looked mildly astonished. 'But if you believe in what you're doing, why should you need to make excuses for it?'

'I am not making excuses,' she raged at him.

He shrugged. 'Typical female, incapable of rational discussion.'

Maren caught the twist of mockery on his mouth and her indignation turned to cold anger. He was deliberately baiting her and like a fool, she had played right into his hands.

'I'm not a typical anything,' she stated. 'And you are in no position to criticise. Discussion requires an open mind, a quality you obviously lack.'

A muscle jumped in his lean jaw. 'And one that you possess?'

'So my colleagues tell me.'

He nodded thoughtfully. 'Tell me, how many women work with you?'

'None. We have –'

He interrupted smoothly, 'So these colleagues you speak of are all men?'

'Obviously, but I don't see what diff –'

'Oh, come on,' he scoffed. 'One woman among a group of men? Don't expect me to believe you're just *one of the boys*.' His voice grew harsh, derisive. 'A woman with your looks could recite the telephone directory and convince every man listening he had just heard something of earth-shattering importance.'

Maren was so bewildered by his animosity that the full import of his words didn't register. She wanted to shout, 'You're wrong. It's not like that at all. They don't see me as a woman. I'm simply a member of the team, one more brain.' But though it was the truth, she knew he wouldn't believe her.

His eyes were diamond hard. 'It must be a pretty important project, this search for a vaccine; the best brains, plenty of funds.'

Maren nodded, rather surprised that he had returned to the subject. 'It is. As well as our lot, there is an enormous amount of work being done in Australia and the United States – and a Nobel Prize for whoever gets there first,' she added ironically.

'A Nobel Prize?' Nicholas sounded impressed. 'Well, I guess that explains why you're involved.' Stung by the bitter jibe, Maren opened her mouth to correct him, to explain that the award hardly mattered. But he gave her no chance. 'I bet there's pretty stiff competition for places on the team?' He still sounded keenly interested. But Maren was beginning to feel uneasy.

'Yes,' she agreed hesitantly. 'Though vacancies don't occur very often.'

They rounded another bend and the track opened out into a rough clearing, littered with leaves and twigs. Several tall thin trees, dead and bare, pointed skyward like skeletal fingers to where thick cloud was piling up in ominous warning.

Nicholas swung the Land Rover to the upper side of the clearing and stopped. 'We'll stay here tonight,' he announced, switching off the engine.

Maren nodded and opened her door. She had thought they were staying at a village. She would ask about that later but right now, all she wanted was to stand on solid ground and stretch her stiff muscles and aching bones.

'Just one thing.'

Maren turned her head to meet Nicholas's calculating gaze. His dark eyes flickered to her mouth, pausing for an instant before sliding down the golden column of her neck to rest on her full breasts, their rounded curves sculpted by the damp, clinging shirt, then to the flare of her hips and back again.

His sensual mouth twisted into a smile, but his eyes were cold and cynical. 'How did *you* do it?'

Puzzlement clouded Maren's face. 'I'm sorry, I don't understand.'

His face hardened. 'How did you get into this exclusive band?'

The inference was plain. Maren's stomach contracted. Now it was only too clear where his questions had been leading. How could he? How dare he?

Swallowing the lump in her throat, she tilted her chin proudly, matching her smile to his. 'I seduced the director, what else?' Then, sliding out of the Land Rover, she slammed the door with all the force she could muster.

She walked to the lower edge of the clearing, resolutely closing her mind to everything but the physical acts of moving her legs, stretching her arms and easing the tension in her shoulders.

As Maren looked down over the hillside she saw, several yards below, a cluster of round huts with thatched roofs. Scrawny chickens scratched in the dirt in front of three of the structures which huddled together on the edge of gardens containing a variety of crops, all in various stages of ripeness.

Further down the hillside the gardens were laid out in neat plots, some divided by bamboo thickets and stands of trees. Two more houses, larger than those in the group, stood apart, backing on to a piece of partly cleared land where three men were cutting down and burning trees and brush.

Another smaller house stood alone on the opposite side of the yard, and behind it a spring bubbled out of the hillside and trickled down in a silver ribbon to vanish into the forest. The whole compound of houses and gardens was surrounded by a fence of upright sticks bound together by plaited reeds, creepers and bark. Maren wondered why, until she caught sight of several pigs rooting about on the partly cleared land. They would soon wreck the crops if they got into the gardens.

Was this the village Nicholas had referred to? She couldn't see anything that she would term a rest house. But as he had so bluntly told her, she didn't know what to look for.

The sound of laughter drew her attention to the grass-skirted women working in the gardens closest to the hamlet. Some were harvesting crops, tossing vegetables and leaves into net bags. Others were planting seeds, using pointed sticks. Children, just out of babyhood, toddled naked among the plants, chased by older girls. Two men, one in ragged shorts, the other wearing a piece of cloth wrapped sarong-style round his hips, were repairing part of the fence near one of the larger houses. Others were picking the fruit in a separate plot planted with chest-high bushes.

A group of boys emerged from the forest carrying bows and arrows and home-made traps, chattering excitedly as they compared catches.

A sudden flurry of squeals and grunts made Maren jump. Six large black pigs, two with white markings, charged out of the forest, pushing and nudging as they scrambled towards the fence near the three houses.

The arrival of the pigs seemed to be a signal for everyone to stop work. The women, laughing and shouting to one another, gathered up tools, children and net bags full of vegetables and began moving up the hillside towards the hamlet.

The men also left what they were doing and those among the bushes lifted reed baskets full of berries onto their heads and started homeward.

'It's coffee.' Maren started at Nicholas's deep voice, unexpectedly close. She had been so engrossed in the scene below she had not heard him approach.

'What is?' She glanced round, but he was studying the little hamlet and she could not read his expression.

'The red berries in those baskets.' He pointed them out to her. 'That's coffee.'

Maren was bemused. It was as though his cynical accusation and her furious retort had never occurred. Well, she could be equally cool. 'Do they sell it?'

Nicholas nodded. 'A buyer comes up from Okapa with a truck. The villagers sell vegetables too. They've established a lucrative market among the Europeans on Papua New Guinea, thanks to Bilas Kanawe.'

'Why? What did he do?' Almost unwillingly Maren's interest was aroused. Despite their turbulent relationship, she found Nicholas's wide knowledge of the country and its people irresistible. She wished she could find out why he was so hostile towards her. But if she asked him directly, she would be revealing that his opinion of her mattered. And that would be giving him the bullets to shoot her with.

It surprised her how much his sudden bursts of bitter antagonism hurt. It shouldn't matter. She ought to be able to shrug them off, ignore them. Yet she couldn't. Was she simply oversensitive? Had she been too long protected from abrasive characters like him by the narrow life she had so far led?

It was true she had little contact with anyone but her family outside her own highly specialised sphere. That had never bothered her before. So why should she care what he thought?

Maren sighed and closed her eyes momentarily. Damn the man. Every time she had tried to rationalise her thoughts and actions since meeting him, she wound up on a state of helpless confusion.

'Am I boring you?'

The sardonic enquiry jolted Maren out of her reverie.

'No,' she answered quickly. It was the truth. He might be insufferably arrogant, unpredictable and harsh, but he certainly wasn't boring. 'Please go on, what did Mr Kanawe do?'

'Do you really care?' He was plainly sceptical.

'I'm interested, yes.' Maren was brusque. 'But I'm not going to plead with you to tell me.' She waited for the sarcastic reply she was sure would come. But, as unpredictable as ever, when Nicholas spoke he merely sounded amused.

'Well, as you're interested, he got together some of the brightest young men from villages around Okapa, showed them how to cultivate tomatoes, onions, cucumbers, peas, cabbages and potatoes, gave them some seeds and sent them home. Within a year, after a hiccup or two, the Europeans were enjoying the same fresh vegetables they would have eaten at home. Come on, we'd better get our gear.' He studied her thoughtfully. 'I hope you still remember something of your basic training.'

Maren refused to rise to the bait. 'Oh? Why?' She calmly switched her gaze to the hamlet below and noticed one woman some way behind the rest, supporting herself with a stick as she stumbled slowly up the hill. No one went to help her and every few minutes she would stop, shaking from head to toe, as if she were cold.

'Because we repay the village's hospitality by holding a surgery,' Nicholas replied, setting off for the Land Rover.

Maren followed him. 'But isn't there an aid post or health centre nearby?'

Nicholas nodded. 'Two miles away across the mountains in the next village.'

'Won't the doctor object if we start treating his patients?'

'What doctor?' Nicholas asked innocently.

Maren sighed in exasperation. What game was he playing now? 'The one at the –' Then it dawned on her. 'You mean there isn't a qualified doctor?'

Nicholas shook his head.

'Not even a nurse?'

Another shake.

'But the books said –'

'You're not that naïve, surely,' he snorted. 'New Guinea has more natural obstacles to development than most places. So even with unlimited funds there would still be enormous problems to overcome before intentions became achievements.'

'Then who does run the aid post?'

'A couple of auxiliaries with a few months' training between them.'

His casual answer irritated Maren. 'Surely there must be someone to whom they can refer?'

Nicholas opened the back door of the Land Rover and hauled out their rucksacks, two sleeping bags rolled up in waterproof sheets, and a white plastic box with a wide shoulder strap.

'The nearest hospital is in Okapa,' he said relocking the door and walking round the vehicle to check the other doors and windows. 'In good conditions that's almost a day's drive away. The doctors there have tried to organise a rota that ensures outlying villages are visited at least once a month.' He slung his rucksack over one shoulder and picked up the sleeping bags which were tied together by string.

'Well, that's something,' Maren began, shrugging on her own pack. 'Even so –'

'However,' Nicholas cut in as he picked up the white box, 'Okapa is an expanding town. Its medical resources are already stretched to the limit. You've seen the state of the only road.' Maren winced at the memory of the miserably uncomfortable ride she had just endured. 'When you take into account that the hamlets and villages here in the south are widely spread and separated by steep mountains and valleys, it's pretty obvious that a regular medical service is simply not possible.'

He started down the narrow muddy path leading from the clearing to the hamlet. Though she knew it was unreasonable, Maren was irked that despite the load he was carrying Nicholas was as agile and sure-footed as a cat. She had a sudden, intense desire to see him trip and fall flat on his face.

He was as much at ease in this wild primitive environment as he would have been in the academic atmosphere of a university, or coping with the high technology of a modern hospital. Why did he have to be so infuriatingly good at everything?

She lifted her gaze from the path to glower in frustration at Nicholas's broad shoulders, remembering against her will the power in his muscular arms and the hardness of his lean, sinewy body.

Without warning she missed her footing and slid down the rough path, cannoning into the back of his legs in an undignified heap.

He remained as steady as a rock and glanced over his shoulder. 'For the third time today, are you all right?' His enquiry was tinged with exasperation.

'I'm fine,' Maren replied flatly. But as she struggled to her feet, ignoring his outstretched hand, the gleam in his eye gave her the uncomfortable feeling he had known exactly what was in her mind.

She brushed herself down, her head lowered to hide the blush that burned her cheeks. Her rear end had certainly taken a lot of punishment over the past few hours.

'You'd better take my hand,' Nicholas warned her. 'This next bit is very steep.'

'I can manage, thanks.' Her refusal was immediate

and instinctive.

'Yes, you've just proved that,' came the dry retort. But before Maren could think of a suitably crushing reply, he switched to cool logic. 'Look, independence and self-sufficiency are all very well. But don't cause unnecessary problems. You sprain your ankle and your trip ends here.'

There was no way she could refuse his proffered hand. Any further argument would not only make him angry, it might start him wondering why she was so anxious to avoid his touch.

As she took his hand she sent up a heartfelt plea that her reluctance was groundless, that she would feel nothing and that the shattering impact of his kiss had been due to shock and fear, nothing else.

But as his strong fingers closed over hers, her heart tripped on an extra beat. The warmth of his firm clasp coursed up her arm, flooding her body with quivering awareness. Their eyes met for an instant and locked. Then in his dark gaze something changed. For a fraction of a second he seemed surprised, almost shaken.

Abruptly he turned away, leading her down the path. He paused every few steps to let her catch up. But not once did he look back. When they reached easier going he released her hand at once.

Maren's own feelings were strangely mixed. There was anger. She could have managed the path on her own, if he had given her a little more time. She hadn't needed his help. His insistence had only been a device to compare his agility with her awkwardness. Surreptitiously she wiped her hand down the side of her trousers, as if by rubbing away the lingering warmth of his touch she could erase the sense of loss.

In the time it had taken them to descend the path, several small fires had been lit in the hamlet yard. Already groups were forming round them as vegetables were peeled and cut, cooking pots and bamboo tubes brought from the houses and water fetched from the spring.

Remembering what Nicholas had told her, Maren was not surprised to see that though the children moved freely between the groups, helping themselves to titbits, men and women remained separate, each sex preparing and cooking its own food.

A girl of about 12 was throwing leaves and vegetable peelings to the waiting pigs. She caught sight of Maren and Nicholas as they made their way through brush and kunai grass to the hamlet.

Her excited cry brought the rest of the villagers to their feet and within minutes, the two of them were surrounded and hustled through the fence into the yard.

The smiles and babble directed at Nicholas told Maren that he was known and welcome. The villagers' reaction to her was more restrained. Curiosity vied with shyness as they chattered among themselves, some sneaking sidelong glances while others stared openly, taking in every detail of her clothes, her figure and her pale skin.

Unused to such scrutiny and conscious of her grubby, dishevelled state, Maren was acutely embarrassed. 'Why do they stare so? What are they saying?' she murmured to Nicholas as he responded to them in their own tongue.

He looked down at her, his face expressionless and

his dark brown eyes curiously opaque. 'They want to know why you are here and if you are my woman.' He turned back to the villagers, leaving Maren speechless, and the alien sounds flowed effortlessly from his lips as he gestured to their fires, to the sky and then to the forest and mountains.

The villagers, whose low foreheads, wide noses and frizzy hair reminded Maren of Aboriginal Australians, began to drift away, back to their chores and their fires, their shouted exchanges punctuated by gales of laughter.

Maren turned to see Nicholas striding in the direction of the small, windowless hut standing alone on the edge of the hamlet. Uncertain of what to do, she hurried to catch up with him. 'Where are we going?'

'To the rest house.'

Maren looked round, her mind filling with vague thoughts of a cool, refreshing shower, a comfortable bed and a nourishing meal, then hours and hours of blissful sleep. 'Where is it?'

Nicholas stopped outside the hut, shrugged the load from his shoulders and began to undo the plaited reed ropes holding the crude door in place. 'Right here.'

Maren stared at the hut with its reed thatch, hanging unevenly over the walls which, like the fence, were made of upright sticks bound together with reeds and thin strips of bark. Horror and disbelief spread over her face chased by acute disappointment.

'You can't be serious,' she whispered, aghast.

'Why not?' he replied calmly. Setting the door

against the wall he stepped inside and swiftly inspected the floor and roof. Then he came out, picked up his rucksack and the sleeping bags and, bending over to avoid hitting his head on the low doorway, he stepped back inside the hut. His voice floated out. 'The roof's a bit low.'

Maren still stood transfixed, refusing to believe he really meant it. It was just a joke, he was teasing her. He had to be.

He came out again, picked up the white box and reached for Maren's rucksack. 'It's a bit awkward, but understandable as there's no one else in the province of my height, but if you –'

'I'm not sleeping in there,' Maren stated flatly, snatching her rucksack out of his reach.

Nicholas straightened up. 'Then where do you propose to sleep?' his deep voice was still pleasant, his tone conversational.

'In the Land Rover,' Maren replied. Thank goodness he was going to be reasonable about it. He must see she couldn't possibly –

'But I have the keys.' He flashed her a smile.

'Yes, I know,' Maren said impatiently then caught herself. She mustn't antagonise him now. Her answering smile was a fraction uncertain. 'If you'll give them to me, I'll go and –'

'No.' It was clear, cold and unequivocal.

'But you can't expect–'

'I can, and I will do whatever I see fit.' His grim expression warned Maren that his own patience was exhausted.

She was past caring. 'I refuse to share this – this – hut with you. It's barely big enough for one person, let alone the two of us.'

'Just a minute,' he cut in. 'There is an alternative.'

'What? What is it?'

Irony twisted to his mouth. 'If my company is so abhorrent, I expect I could persuade the women to let you share one of their houses.'

Maren stared at him then spun round to look at the women busy cooking at their fires while girls and toddlers wandered in and out of the cluster of three huts, which were hardly much bigger than the one behind her.

'It would be very cramped, of course. But I'm sure you wouldn't object. After all you are a woman, just like them. I'll go and arrange it.' He started forward, moving her aside with a careless gesture.

'No.' The word came from Maren's throat in a strangled whisper.

Nicholas stopped and swung round. 'I beg your pardon? What was that? I didn't hear you.' He was utterly merciless.

Maren moistened her lips with a parched tongue. 'I said no,' she repeated harshly, looking him full in the face, flinching under his stony gaze.

'You don't want to share a house with the women?'

Driven beyond endurance, Maren turned on Nicholas. 'No, I don't!' she shouted at him, heedless of the villagers' startled glances. Words poured from her in a torrent of anger and frustration. 'I don't want to sleep with those savages, and I don't want to sleep with you. I'm filthy, I'm hungry and I'm tired. A bath and food I'll manage without, but I'm damned if I'll let myself be blackmailed into –'

'Be quiet.' His eyes were as hard as flint in a face like thunder. 'I have never laid a finger on a woman in anger but by God, if you don't stop behaving like a spoilt brat –' He broke off, controlling himself with an obvious effort. 'It is a house we are to share, not a bed.' His icy contempt made Maren flush to the roots of her hair. 'Now give me your rucksack and –' He stopped speaking as his gaze switched to something behind her. Seeing his expression change, Maren turned.

Two girls carrying armfuls of huge fern fronds slipped behind her into the hut, emerging seconds later without them. Another girl was following, her soft face furrowed in concentration as she carried funnel-shaped leaves containing steaming food towards them. Reaching them she smiled shyly and offered the food to Maren.

Maren looked at the mess on the leaves. It was unrecognisable. Her nerves stretched to breaking point by weariness and the stress of the day, Maren's stomach heaved in rebellion.

The girl darted a glance at Nicholas, her face clouding with dismay and disappointment as she tentatively offered the food once more.

Maren attempted a shaky smile. 'It's very kind of you,' she began. 'But I –'

'Take it,' Nicholas growled.

She threw him a pleading glance. 'Please, I can't – '

'Take it,' he repeated, his tone threatening dire consequences if she did not obey.

Maren held out her hands and the girl carefully placed her gift into them. Then flashing them both a grin of pure delight, she scampered away, her shy formality replaced by childish glee as she joined her two friends in a welter of giggles and whispers.

Maren watched them for a moment then her eyes fell to her hands and she burned with shame.

She had called them savages. Yet they had welcomed her, a total stranger, with food, shelter and, she remembered, the ferns, a soft bed. Would she have done the same for them?

She forced herself to look at Nicholas. His implacable face might have been carved from stone.

'Get inside,' he said.

Chapter Six

Bending her head, Maren stepped carefully through the narrow opening. Nicholas followed, his muscular shoulders blocking the light for a moment. He tossed her rucksack into the pile of ferns on the earth floor. She could feel the anger emanating from him. But before he could open his mouth she turned, her head brushing the roof.

'I want to apologise.' Her voice wobbled and she had to clear her throat before she could go on.

Nicholas was silent. The fast-fading light illuminated half his face, but the other half was in deep shadow. He did not help her. He simply watched and waited.

'I should not have said – wh – what I did. It was stupid and ungrateful of me and I –' She faltered. 'I'm ashamed.'

Nicholas did not reply immediately. When he did, he did not refer to her stumbling apology.

'Sit down,' he ordered, 'right where you are. Put the food down, there in the light from the doorway.' He crouched beside her and she had to assume the incident was closed, for the moment. 'I will tell you what is on each banana leaf and you will taste it.'

'Please, Nicholas,' Maren begged, using his name

without thinking, 'I can't. I'm not used to –'

'Just a minute,' he cut in quietly. 'What did you imagine we'd be living on during this expedition?'

Maren opened her mouth. Then closed it again.

'Did you expect a hotel at each stop? Sandwich bars? A takeaway?'

'No, of course not,' she snorted.

'Then what?' he pressed.

'Oh, I don't know.' Maren shrugged in exasperation. 'I didn't think –'

'Quite,' came his dry response. 'You are remarkably adept at that.' He gave her no time to reply. Picking up a long white vegetable, he broke a piece off. The flesh steamed as he broke it again. He popped one piece into his mouth and put the other to her lips. Instinctively Maren recoiled.

'Open your mouth or I'll force-feed you,' he warned.

Realising he would not hesitate to carry out his threat, she opened her mouth, feeling faintly ridiculous as he placed the vegetable on her tongue. Gingerly she began to chew. It had a crumbly texture and a bland floury taste.

'That is sweet potato.' He didn't wait for her to ask. 'It has replaced taro as the staple food of the Highlanders. Though there are about seventy varieties, each hamlet usually only grows ten or twelve.' He lifted a green and white vegetable that reminded Maren of asparagus or leek. 'This is pit-pit, the heart of a thick-stemmed grass. Try it, it's quite succulent.' She did and it was.

'What's that?' She pointed to a small but solid mass of dark green leaves. 'It looks like spinach.'

86

'Kumu.'

Maren nibbled some without waiting to be told. She had to admit this wasn't quite as bad as she had feared. 'They obviously have a large variety of vegetables, but what do they do for protein?'

Nicholas swallowed the mouthful he was chewing before he answered. 'Pigs are the main source. Pig feasts cement political alliances between hamlets, settle disputes and debts, pay bride-prices and celebrate initiations, marriages and funerals. The Fore usually eat pig meat two or three times a month, though after a ceremonial feast it can be several days a week. There is a special pig-exchange feast which takes place every few years when over a hundred pigs may be killed.'

While Nicholas was talking Maren had been cautiously helping herself from some of the other leaves. 'Who looks after all those pigs?' she asked, nibbling on a mixture she recognised as sweetcorn and mushrooms.

'Traditionally the women did. They treated the pigs like pets, even sharing their houses with them.'

Maren's head came up. She wasn't sure if he was joking. Nicholas saw her doubt.

'It's quite true. Now they are fenced out of the hamlets. Since human contact with them has lessened due to government influence, the men have become more involved in their care. But the women used to look after their pigs as we would a cat or dog, grooming them regularly, allowing them free run of the hamlet, and generally regarding them with great affection as very desirable companions.' Nicholas helped himself to pieces of light-coloured meat.

Absorbed in what he was telling her, Maren did the same.

Nicholas paused for a moment, watching her, but Maren did not notice.

'Well,' she said, chewing thoughtfully, 'I suppose they were a sort of instant waste disposal.' She smiled and shook her head, licking her fingers.

'What's funny?'

Maren grimaced. 'Me. Sitting in a grass hut, using my fingers to eat chunks of chicken and vegetables I've never heard of, and discussing pigs as house pets. If Russell had told me it would be like this –'

'You wouldn't have come,' Nicholas stated.

'Yes, I would …' she began, only to falter as his steady gaze challenged her. 'Well, maybe I –'

'Just think what you'd have missed,' he grinned, his teeth startlingly white in the gloom.

Maren's heart lurched and she caught her breath, quickly looking down at the food. He smiled so rarely, but when he did its effect on her was devastating.

'By the way –' his deep voice held no particular inflection '– that wasn't chicken.'

Maren looked up at him. 'What was it then? Pork?' Her brows drew together in a frown as she stared suspiciously at the remaining slivers of meat on the leaf then switched her gaze to Nicholas.

He shook his head. 'Some of it was snake, python, to be precise, and a few witchetty grubs. They are the larvae of the longicorn beetle. The Fore regard them as a great delicacy.'

Maren's eyes widened and her hand flew to her mouth, then to her stomach. 'Oh, you –' she started to scramble to her feet. But he was too quick for her. Leaning forward, he grabbed both her arms.

'Let go of me,' she cried, trying to break his grip, 'I'm going to be sick.'

'No you're not,' he replied firmly, and the bruising pressure of his strong fingers tightened as she struggled.

'That was a rotten thing to do!' she flung at him. 'You should have told me.' She wrenched one hand free. The sudden movement caught Nicholas off balance and he keeled over sideways onto the ferns.

Unable to free her other hand Maren toppled backwards. Though the pile of greenery cushioned her landing, the force was enough to knock her breathless.

Gasping and furious she lashed out, catching Nicholas a stinging blow on the side of his head that made her fingers ache. 'You rotten, lousy – it's all a huge joke to you, isn't it?' She tried to hit him again. 'A great laugh at my expense –'

Nicholas flung himself forward and as he sprawled half-across her, pinning her down on the ferns, he seized her free hand and forced them both above her head. 'Stop it,' he grated. 'Stop it at once.'

The brief, bitter struggle had sapped the last of Maren's strength. Bathed in a dew of perspiration, unable to move, her heart pounded a wild rhythm in her ears. She turned her head to see Nicholas's dark eyes, narrowed and glittering, only inches from hers.

'I did tell you,' he growled, the words coming from deep in his throat.

Though less painful, Maren's breathing was still ragged and now she had stopped struggling she could feel the strong, steady thud of his heart against her breast. His sweat-soaked shirt was plastered to him like a second skin. Through the thin material his weight pressed down, moulding her body to his, making her burningly aware of every contour of his hard-muscled torso.

'I – m – meant that you should have told me first,' she stammered. 'Before I ate it.' Something strange was happening to her. Her anger was fading, trickling away like sand through her fingers. Lassitude stole over her, draining the tension from her limbs, leaving them heavy and languorous.

Above her, the harsh planes of Nicholas's face blurred.

'Had I told you first, you wouldn't have touched it, would you?' His voice was a low vibrating rumble that Maren felt rather than heard. She was drifting, helpless on a slow surging tide. She tried to answer but the only sound to come from her lips was a soft sigh. A shudder ran through Nicholas and his body tensed. His low groan brought her to her senses with shocking suddenness.

Her eyes flew open. She could not mistake the hunger that burned in his gaze and tightened his features. Her body had betrayed her. The realisation appalled Maren. In a torment of shame and embarrassment she arched her body in a desperate effort to throw him off.

'Let me up,' she demanded, her voice cracking in alarm.

Lightning-fast, he pressed her down again, crushing her into the ferns, forcing a gasp from her parted lips as liquid fire surged through her veins.

'Why?' he demanded softly, rearing above her, his hooded gaze straying to her mouth.

'No,' she whispered as his head came down. 'No, don't, please don't.' She began to struggle violently, thrashing her head from side to side, so that his mouth should not reach hers. She was torn by the battle raging inside her. He wanted her, the throbbing pressure of his body against her was undeniable proof of that. And the clamour of her own need had been almost irresistible. But it was all wrong. How could this man have stirred her so? They were not lovers, they were not even friends.

'Get off me,' she cried hoarsely, 'let me up.' Stunned and terrified by his power to sweep her so quickly to such dizzy, voluptuous heights, Maren fought like a madwoman, her breath exploding in choking sobs.

She did not see desire fade from Nicholas's face, replaced by a puzzled frown. She only knew that suddenly his weight had gone and her hands were free.

Rolling over, Maren drew her knees up to her chest and sat hunched against the wall trembling uncontrollably. Her hair had come loose and fell about her shoulders in a wild tangle.

'What is it? Did I hurt you?' Kneeling a few feet away, Nicholas's tone was a blend of bewilderment, frustration and concern.

Maren shook her head, pushing her hair back from her face with a shaking hand. 'No,' she croaked, sucking in deep breaths, trying to calm her heart's frantic thudding.

'Then why such a struggle?' his voice hardened.

'You don't expect me to believe that's the first time a man has tried to make love to you.'

'No,' Maren said again. She didn't expect him to believe anything she said.

'I guessed as much.' He laughed a brief bitter sound. 'A woman with your advantages would hardly be lacking experience.' Having stuck the knife in, he proceeded to twist it. 'How many lovers have you had? Ten? Twenty?'

'That is none of your business,' Maren replied tightly, pretending calm, refusing to acknowledge the lacerating pain his contemptuous allegations were causing. 'You have no right to ask that question and even less to expect an answer.'

'Touché,' Nicholas inclined his head in sardonic salute. 'But you still haven't explained the frightened virgin act.'

Maren's brain was racing. It would be foolish to deny his ability to arouse her, he had just received all too obvious proof of that. But she was too shaken by her own reactions and much too unsure of him to reveal the whole truth: that there had been no string of lovers, that he had opened her unwilling eyes to the fact that her one affair, with Paul, had been merely a milestone on her road to maturity and not the grand passion she had believed it to be. Through Nicholas she was at last free from the cage of hurt and suspicion which had imprisoned her for so long. It was he who had unknowingly extinguished the lingering traces of girlhood and kindled within her the glorious, incandescent fire of a woman's sensuality.

She could tell him none of it, for he believed her to be a sophisticated, experienced woman.

'Well?'

She had run out of time. He wanted an answer and he wanted it now. 'It's quite simple,' she said casually, 'I changed my mind. It's a woman's prerogative, remember?'

'You changed your mind?' he repeated slowly.

Tossing her hair back, Maren paused as she brushed bits of broken fern from her trousers. 'Oh dear, have I hurt your pride?' she asked with exaggerated concern. 'Have you never been turned down before?'

His mouth tightened and Maren resumed the mechanical actions of tidying herself, avoiding his gaze. With enormous effort she kept her voice as light as a soufflé.

'OK, so there was a certain physical chemistry –' A tongue of flame leapt, white-hot, within her. Her legs turned to water and her heart lurched erratically at the vivid memory of his powerful body covering hers, pressing her down onto the bed of ferns.

Head bent, her hair falling like a curtain across her face, Maren closed her eyes briefly. Careful, she must be careful. She must not reveal more than he himself had noticed. 'But it's hardly significant.' She shrugged, in a convincing show of indifference. 'A man, a woman,' she gestured vaguely, 'all this …'

'I see,' he interrupted. 'You mean it was simply a matter of biology, exaggerated by circumstances, the unusual environment and so on.'

'Yes,' Maren agreed, 'that's it exactly. But of course it doesn't mean anything.'

'Ah.'

Maren darted him a sideways glance. He was

studying her thoughtfully.

'So, your frenzied efforts to get away from me, your pallor –' he brushed her cheek lightly with a forefinger, his touch a trail of fire that lingered long after his hand had gone '– the shakes you are trying so hard to disguise, are all because it didn't mean anything?'

'I don't know what you're talking about.' Maren moistened her dry lips with the tip of her tongue. 'I'm tired, it's been a long day,' she blustered. 'Look, as you're obviously determined to misunderstand, you leave me no choice but to be brutally frank.'

'Oh, please go ahead,' Nicholas urged.

Maren bit her lip. He made everything so difficult. 'All right, here it is.' She took a deep breath. 'Forget any ideas of an affair. I simply don't find you attractive enough.' There, she had said it. Now surely his pride would keep him at a distance.

Nicholas rose to his feet with pantherlike smoothness, keeping his head and shoulders bent to avoid the roof. He paused, staring down at her. 'You are lying,' he said softly. 'I wonder why?' He picked up a wooden bucket standing by the doorway. 'Stay here. I'll fetch some water for you to wash.' He was gone before Maren could utter a word.

She was still there, leaning against the wall, her thoughts spinning like a whirlpool, when he returned a few minutes later.

'I'm going to talk to the men,' he announced, placing the full bucket on the earth floor. 'They might know more than Bilas about the fighting. I'll be about half an hour. There's a torch in the front pocket of my pack.' With that he disappeared once more.

Pushing herself away from the wall, Maren crawled to the doorway and looked out. The sun had set, its final rays hidden by thick cloud that blanketed the mountain peaks. Darkness was settling with incredible speed over the hamlet. The fires were dying. But still some of the villagers sat, reluctant to leave the glowing embers while they yet offered warmth in the swiftly cooling air. Nicholas sat with them.

Maren shivered. Her damp clothes were clammy and uncomfortable. At least he'd had the decency to allow her a little time to herself. But to do all that she wanted before he returned, she would have to hurry.

Feeling her way to Nicholas's pack, almost knocking the bucket over as she went, Maren found the torch. It seemed to be sealed inside a polythene bag. She was about to try and tear the bag off, when she realised that it was there for protection against rain and humidity.

She switched it on through the film and shone it round the hut, glancing nervously up at the roof. A lizard darted, a flash of silvery-green, into the kunai grass thatch. In the apex of the cone-shaped roof, a large, black spider crouched in the centre of a glistening web. Maren shuddered and turned the beam onto her rucksack. She could do nothing about the other inhabitants of the hut, so it was better not to know what, where, or how many they were.

A pattering sound caught her attention and she stopped rummaging for her toilet bag to listen. It grew faster and louder. Then she let her breath out in a sigh of relief as she realised the rain had begun. Crawling to the opening Maren reached outside and pulled the crude door across the hole, leaving it unfastened so that Nicholas would be able to get in later.

Just for an instant she considered tying it in place from the inside. He could go and sleep with the men. The temptation was very strong. But as she turned to crawl back to her rucksack, Maren knew that if he came back to find the door barred against him, he was quite likely to tear the hut apart with his bare hands. What he would do to her then did not bear contemplation.

Jamming the torch into a strand of plaited bark fibre which bound together the upright stakes forming the walls, Maren pushed her rucksack to one side. Quickly dividing the pile of ferns she gathered up one half and flung them to the other side of the hut, then she dragged Nicholas's pack over beside them. If they had to share the hut, it would be at the greatest possible distance.

Unfastening the sleeping bags she threw one, and a waterproof sheet, onto his fern pile and tossed the others onto her own. She would sort it out properly later. Right now, more than anything else, she wanted a wash.

Carefully, so that the water did not slop over the sides, Maren manoeuvred the bucket into the space between the fern piles. Then, pulling a towel and fresh shirt from her rucksack, she piled them on top of it, hopefully out of reach of any small creatures looking for new places to live. After one more tentative glance round and an adjustment to the torch, so that the beam shone onto the bucket and not onto her, Maren twisted her hair into a knot on top of her head and unbuttoned her shirt.

As she soaped herself, leaning over the bucket to rinse off the lather, the water, cold and silky soft, trickled in rivulets over her breasts, sparkling diamond-bright in the torchlight. She shivered as the night air struck cold on her wet skin.

But much to her own amazement, instead of hating the discomfort, Maren found herself smiling. This was certainly nothing like the bath she had envisaged. There was precious little comfort to be found in the crude hut.

Yet though she was bruised and weary her senses seemed somehow sharper. There was a startling clarity to the spring water's icy bite, the velvet smoothness of the lather, the musty smell of the thatch, the ferns' acrid pungency and the soft, insistent patter of the rain.

She plunged her arm into the water then held it high in the torchlight. A rainbow danced in each drop of water as it fell from her fingers. She felt strange, different. It was as though she had been stripped of an outer skin, which while protecting her from hurt or distraction had also clouded her consciousness of the world about her.

Her arrival in this exotic, primitive land had marked the beginning of a journey of discovery into herself. Not knowing where it would lead, or what she would find, she felt terrifyingly vulnerable. Yet she could not stop, and there was no going back.

The sound of running footsteps jolted her out of her reverie. She just had time to slip her arms into her clean shirt before Nicholas pushed the door aside and squeezed into the hut. Rain had darkened his shirt and glistened in his hair.

'Aren't you finished yet?' he growled impatiently and Maren was glad the dim light hid her scarlet face and trembling hands as she tried to button her shirt with fingers that had all become thumbs. 'Yes, I've finished,' she managed at last. 'Would you like me to wait outside while you –'

'What on earth for?' Nicholas reached for his waterproof sheet, slung it around his shoulders, picked up the bucket and turned to the door. 'Pass me the torch, will you? I can't see a damn thing in this rain.'

'Where are you going?' Maren pushed her soap and flannel into her toilet bag then shook out her towel. Of course he needed the torch, but so did she. Why hadn't it occurred to her to bring one of her own? Because she hadn't had the faintest idea of just how primitive conditions would be. She certainly had a few bones to pick with Russell the next time they met.

'To the spring for fresh water.' He grinned, and above the torch beam his eyes gleamed wickedly. 'Sorry to leave you in the dark, but the hut is hardly big enough for you to get lost in.' He turned to go.

'Just a minute,' Maren blurted, hating having to ask, but aware of a growing need. 'Where's the – I mean, where does one –?'

'Behind that clump of bushes down by the fence,' he pointed. 'Wait till I get back and I'll take you down.'

'No,' Maren said hurriedly. 'No, it's quite all right, I'll find it.'

'Please yourself,' Nicholas turned away. 'It's a deep pit with branches either side to stand on. If you keep up today's form and fall in, you'll have to get yourself out. Men are forbidden to go there.'

'Of course I shan't fall in,' Maren said crossly. But he had already gone.

Stuffing her feet into her boots, she draped her waterproof sheet over her head. She hesitated. Should she put her trousers on too? No, it would take precious seconds she could not afford if she was to be back and in her sleeping bag before he returned.

She felt her way to the door and stepped outside. Now her eyes were adjusting she could just make out the solid black shapes of bushes and trees. With small, uncertain steps she made her way carefully across the hamlet yard. Fires had been lit inside some of the houses. As none of them had chimneys or even a hole through which the smoke could escape, Maren wondered how the occupants could even breathe let alone see each other.

Which clump of bushes was it? There were several. Maren tried the nearest. Twigs caught at the sheet and scratched her legs. There was no way through. Cursing Nicholas under her breath, she shuffled towards the next one, screwing her eyes up against the rain, straining to see and avoid bumps and hollows underfoot. Of course it would have been easier with the torch. But it would have been far too embarrassing to have had Nicholas accompany her. Did he have no sensitivity?

This time she found a gap. Wrinkling her nose against the smell, and feeling distinctly unsafe, Maren negotiated the branches in and out again without mishap.

As she retraced her steps the rain grew heavier,

bouncing off the ground. It seemed ages before she reached the hut. She had almost panicked, thinking she'd missed it, when she saw a light shining through the chinks in the wooden wall. Nicholas had returned before her.

Maren paused uncertainly. What should she do? The rain was coming down in torrents. The day's heat was just a memory as a damp chill began to invade her. She couldn't possibly stay out in this, but the prospect of re-entering the hut wearing only briefs and a shirt to face Nicholas in the middle of a bath and quite possibly stark naked, made her hesitate.

Where was her detachment, her objectivity? For heaven's sake, she was a doctor. She knew all there was to know about human bodies. There were only two sexes. If you weren't one, you had to be the other, so why the fuss?

Because theoretical knowledge and personal experience were two entirely different things. And being objective about Nicholas Calder was not easy. In fact, it was impossible. He was overpowering, he unnerved her, yet she was magnetised by him.

'Are you going to hang about out there all night?' Nicholas roared, making Maren jump. How could he have heard her above the drumming rain? She shivered, and it wasn't entirely from cold. 'Maren?' he bellowed.

Why hadn't she taken those few extra seconds to put her trousers on? She tugged ineffectually at her shirt, but it simply would not stretch below her hips.

She stepped inside the hut, careful not to look at him and turned to shake the sheet out of the doorway, reflecting wryly how typical it was that the first time he'd used her name it was in irritation. Suddenly, ridiculously, her eyes filled with tears. She blinked them away, furiously shaking the sheet.

'It's going to be wetter than when you started if you wave it about much longer,' Nicholas remarked.

Maren gave the sheet one last defiant flick then pulled it inside, dropping it in a heap as she replaced the door.

'You've got mud all over your legs,' he said casually, and as she twisted round to look, he spun her in a half-circle. Crouching beside her as she grabbed his bare shoulder to keep her balance, he ran his soapy hand over both her calves.

She leapt away from him, seized her towel and fiercely rubbed her legs dry, her heart hammering as she cursed herself for overreacting.

'For God's sake stop behaving as though I'm rapist of the month,' Nicholas said angrily. His voice grew bitter. 'Contrary to popular belief, my mind does occasionally rise above my navel.'

Maren was defensive. 'You startled me. Anyway I'm quite capable of washing my own legs.'

Ignoring her completely, he bent over the bucket and continued washing.

As she eased past, Maren found it hard to tear her eyes from the muscles bunching and flexing beneath his gleaming, mahogany skin.

Nicholas looked up suddenly. His raised eyebrows and twisted smile told her he was well aware of her scrutiny.

Confused and angry with herself and him, she turned away at once. Spreading her waterproof over the ferns, she unrolled her sleeping bag, kicked off her boots, and climbed in.

As she unpinned her hair and raked a brush through it, she heard him empty the bucket outside and fasten the door in place. Quickly she dropped the brush into one of her boots and wriggled down in her sleeping bag, turning her back to him. She heard him remove his trousers, and a few moments later the crackle and rustle of the ferns under his weight as he zipped up his sleeping bag.

'Goodnight.' Nicholas switched off the torch.

'Goodnight,' Maren replied tightly. The whole situation was simply ludicrous. Here she was, bedding down for the night on a pile of vegetation in a hut made of sticks and grass with a man that 36 hours ago she hadn't even known existed.

Maren turned onto her back and stared into the darkness. Rain pattered on the thatch above and drummed on the earth outside. She could hear Nicholas's breathing, slow and even. Despite her exhaustion she couldn't relax. The hut must be literally crawling with insects. She turned over. Thank heaven the altitude was too great for mosquitoes. Even so, there would be spiders and beetles and almost certainly fleas. She would be eaten alive before morning.

She turned over again. They didn't seem to be bothering Nicholas. But then, they wouldn't. He was obviously used to living rough. No fleas would dare bite him. They'd break their teeth on his thick hide, Maren thought venomously, and was instantly undermined by doubt.

Why had he reacted so bitterly over her muddy legs? He had no right to blame her for acting as she did. She wasn't used to such intimate gestures, especially from a man she barely knew.

But he doesn't know that, a warning voice reminded her. In his opinion you are used to a great deal more.

Maren's head was beginning to ache. She drew her legs up. Why had she started this ridiculous charade? Why hadn't she told him the truth, regardless of the consequences? He might have refused to believe her and she couldn't have done a thing about it. But at least she would have been free of this dreadful burden of pretending to be something she wasn't.

An unearthly squeal rent the air. Maren gasped in sheer fright, her heart in her mouth. She froze, too terrified to move. There was another squeal, followed by loud snorting and grunting. It was only the pigs. She felt almost sick with relief. How was she ever going to survive this trip?

'Relax, woman,' Nicholas said softly, his deep voice surprisingly gentle. 'You're quite safe.'

Still puzzling over whether he meant from the animals or from him, Maren sank into a restless, uneasy sleep.

Chapter Seven

When Maren opened her eyes the following morning, it was several moments before she could remember where she was. Her sleep had been filled with vivid, unfinished dreams and though she could not recall them in detail, they had left behind a sense of bewilderment and vulnerability that weighed heavily.

As the happenings of the previous day flooded back she sat up quickly and winced. All her joints were stiff and her back ached. Pushing her hair off her face, Maren rolled her head from side to side to ease the tightness in her neck and shoulders. Then she saw Nicholas.

He was sitting on his rolled-up sleeping bag, fingers linked, elbows resting on his knees, watching her, a pensive frown deepening the lines between his dark, heavy eyebrows.

Maren's face grew warm under his thoughtful scrutiny. 'Am I late? Have I overslept? You should have woken me.'

Nicholas stretched. 'There's no panic,' he said calmly. 'You obviously needed the sleep. Out here in the wilds timetables tend to be very flexible. In any case we don't leave here until the rain stops.'

Maren looked out of the doorway into the grey

gloom of morning. Rain seemed too mild a word to describe the deluge pouring from a leaden sky.

'There's fresh water in the bucket.' Nicholas nodded towards it, then, taking a battery-powered razor from his pack he turned his back to her and began to shave.

Maren realised that this was as much privacy as she was going to get. She could hardly expect him to stand outside in that torrent. And he had fetched the water for her. He had even waited till she awoke before switching on his razor. She was grateful and rather surprised. Tact was not a characteristic she would have associated with him.

Unzipping her sleeping bag she quickly slid her legs into her trousers. Wriggling them up over her hips she tucked in her shirt and fastened zipper and button all in the space of a few seconds. She pulled on her socks and boots then washed her face and hands and brushed her hair, securing it in a ponytail with a rubber band.

Nicholas's razor stopped buzzing as she turned and knelt to roll up her sleeping bag.

'Do you want hot or cold breakfast?' he asked from behind her. 'Though I warn you, if I light a fire in here you'll know what it is to be a kipper within a couple of hours.'

'Please don't bother on my account,' Maren said quickly, pushing her toilet bag into her rucksack and hauling out a sweater which she put on over her shirt. It was much cooler than yesterday. 'I don't normally eat breakfast anyway.'

'Out here you do,' Nicholas replied firmly and one glance at his face convinced Maren that any argument would be a waste of breath and time. She had to admit the circumstances were rather different from normal and, if she were honest, at his mention of food she had discovered she was surprisingly hungry. Maybe he was right this time.

'We shared my food on the way here yesterday. So if you still have yours I'd like fruit and bread if you have any,' she replied with equal firmness. If he said she must eat, then she would eat. He knew how to prepare for and tackle conditions on an expedition like this and she did not.

It occurred to her that retaining even a trace of independence in the face of his powerful personality and infinitely wider experience was going to be a constant uphill struggle. But it was one she would have to win if she intended to survive this trip as an individual.

Nicholas opened the plastic container he had taken from his pack. 'Mango, pineapple, bananas and bread rolls.' He paused, opening a separately wrapped package. 'And cold roast pork.' He put the container down on the earth between them and gestured for Maren to help herself.

She sat down cross-legged on her sleeping bag and reached for a mango, a banana and a bread roll. 'Do you have a knife, please?'

Nicholas dug into his pocket and produced a black- handled penknife. He opened the largest blade and passed the knife to her. 'It's very sharp,' he warned.

Maren gave him a look. How did he think she managed with scalpels? She cut the mango into quarters and, after handing the knife back with murmured thanks, began to eat. The fruit was delicious, firm but ripe, and so full of juice it trickled down her chin and she had to catch the drops in her palm.

'No meat?' Nicholas asked, slicing the pineapple.

Her mouth still full, Maren could only shake her head.

'If you don't fancy pork, I dare say I could find a chunk of python or a few fat witchetty grubs,' he offered with a perfectly straight face.

Maren studied the bread roll as though it were an object of immense interest before breaking it in half, then raising her eyes to his. He was teasing her. But this was not the contemptuous derision of yesterday. This was different, a sort of testing-the-water-with-a-toe kind of teasing. She matched his seriousness. 'You're too kind. But I've decided to become a vegetarian.'

'A sudden decision, isn't it?'

'Certainly not,' Maren retorted. 'I made it –' she glanced at her watch '– all of 14 hours ago.'

He pointed the knife at her. 'You're not being logical,' he said, and cut himself another slice of pineapple.

'Oh really?' Maren finished the mango. 'Apart from the fact that I'm female, which makes me illogical to start with, what other reason have you for that statement?' She dried her hands and wiped her mouth.

Nicholas swallowed the pineapple he was chewing and leaned forward slightly. 'You were enjoying the meat while you thought it was chicken. It wasn't until I revealed its true identity that you panicked. That proves it wasn't the actual meat you were rejecting. It was an association of ideas that upset you.'

Maren looked up at him. A wayward lock of his black hair hung like a question mark over his forehead. The creases at the sides of his mouth deepened as his lips curved in a quizzical smile. His eyes were very dark and as she looked into them her heart lurched and her mouth was suddenly dry as she remembered what had occurred after that revelation. She could not look away, reliving every moment of their fight with an intensity that was part ecstasy, part pain.

Nicholas's eyebrows lifted a fraction and she realised he had intended her to remember. Suddenly his words took on a new and startling significance. Was he talking about the food, or was he referring to her behaviour, her reaction to him?

She was suddenly frightened. She had always been a very private person. Neither her family nor her closest friends had ever been permitted to share her innermost feelings, her fears, her longings, her self-doubt.

But this man, still almost a stranger, had seen through a façade she had thought impregnable. True, she had duped him at first. Then like a fool she had been upset that he had taken her at face value. But something had changed all that. He had seen a crack, a flaw, and had swooped on it like an eagle onto a rabbit.

What would he do with his discovery? It gave him yet another advantage. How would he use it?

All this flashed through her mind in a few brief seconds. She broke eye contact, her long lashes veiling her eyes. Confused and uncertain she pulled crumbs from the broken roll.

Now she was no longer held in the grip of his gaze, her fear subsided. Surely by telling her in this roundabout way he was giving her the option of taking his words solely at face value. That must mean he did not wish to pressure her.

Then doubt crept in. Perhaps there had not been any hidden message. Had she seen something that wasn't there? Even worse, what if it were her thoughts, her wishes she was projecting onto his words?

'You've heard of the Russian physiologist, Pavlov?' Nicholas asked.

Maren raised her head, surprised. 'Yes. He pioneered the study of human mental disorders. But what –'

Nicholas interrupted her. 'He began his work using dogs. Every time he fed them he rang a bell. The dogs came to associate the bell with food. Eventually, even when the dogs couldn't see or smell food, their mouths would still water when they heard the bell.'

'Yes, I remember. He called it a conditioned reflex.' Maren's forehead puckered, 'But I still –'

'It applies equally to humans,' Nicholas cut in, his deep voice quiet, his gaze mesmeric, challenging. 'How a person responds to a situation depends very much on their past experiences of a similar situation. Do you follow me?'

Maren nodded slowly, her doubts evaporating. She had been right. 'Yes,' she murmured, 'I understand.'

Their eyes remained locked a moment longer, then both looked away at the same instant.

While Nicholas peeled a banana Maren, suddenly ravenous, tore off a piece of her bread roll and began to chew, reflecting that in the short time since she had woken up their relationship had changed yet again. How it would develop she neither knew nor cared. It was enough for the moment that they shared an unspoken understanding, and that the tension between them had eased.

They ate in silence, each immersed in their own thoughts.

Maren finished the bread and twisted round to pull the bottle of Perrier water out of her rucksack. She was unscrewing the top when the question leapt at her. *To which of them had Nicholas been referring?*

She had assumed it was her; that her reactions had been conditioned by events in the past. But what if he had meant himself? If he had, things that had happened the previous day would begin to make sense.

There was the expression on Nicholas's face when he had first seen her in the hotel lobby. She shivered. She would not forget that look in a hurry. Then there had been Dave Edridge's undeniable amazement when he had realised she would be travelling with Nicholas, and the way he had so hastily changed the subject. Even Bilas Kanawe had seemed more curious and surprised than the situation had warranted.

'What's the matter? Something wrong?'

He had eyes like a hawk. Did he ever miss a thing? 'No, nothing. Is the rain likely to last long?'

Nicholas looked out through the open doorway, where rainwater dripped off the uneven thatch in continuous streams. 'It's hard to say. I certainly hope not. We've had a few long spells of rain lately. If it doesn't stop soon it will cause us problems.'

'Such as?' Maren raised the bottle to her lips and drank deeply.

'Swollen streams and rivers, washed-out bridges,' Nicholas replied. 'Also, after several days' rain the remainder of this track has an unpleasant habit of slipping away down the mountainside under the weight of heavy vehicles.'

'Would us in the Land Rover count as a heavy vehicle?' Maren was only half-joking as she tried to ignore an instant, mind's-eye picture of their vehicle rolling and bouncing down an almost vertical slope amid earth, rocks and mud, with bodies and equipment flying out of the crazily flapping doors to be swallowed up by the forest hundreds of feet below. She swallowed convulsively. 'Would you like a drink?' She thrust the bottle at him.

Nicholas took it, examining it. 'I was less than polite about this yesterday.'

'Yes, you were,' Maren agreed. His black head came up quickly. 'Aren't you lucky I don't bear grudges?' She had to bite the inside of her lower lip to prevent herself from smiling openly at his astonishment, quickly masked, but not before she had enjoyed the small ripple of satisfaction his reaction had given her.

He said nothing, merely raising the bottle in salute before putting it to his lips and watching her through narrowed eyes as he drank. His look had the effect of an electric shock and Maren felt her nerve ends tingle. She quickly began collecting all the fruit peel together, piling it into the plastic box.

111

Nicholas handed the bottle back. She took it without looking up, murmuring her thanks, busily brushing crumbs off her trousers.

'I'll take this lot out to the pigs,' he said, getting to his feet and picking up the box. He reached for the bucket. 'I might as well deal with that at the same time.'

Maren put out a hand to stop him. 'Could I just clean my teeth first?'

'What are you going to use? This water's dirty.'

She held up the bottle.

He put the bucket down again and grinned. 'That's about all it's fit for.'

Maren rummaged for her toilet bag, got out her toothbrush and squeezed paste onto it. She darted him a glance. 'You know your trouble?'

He crouched opposite her. 'I've a suspicion you're going to tell me,' his eyes gleamed.

Maren sighed elaborately. 'You just don't appreciate the finer things in life.' Her mouth tilted in an impish grin.

Nicholas's face remained stony for a moment then he started to laugh.

Maren's heart gave an odd leap. She began to brush her teeth, keeping her head down, knowing she would be unable to hide the sudden rush of happiness that bubbled inside her. As she rinsed her mouth he took the bottle from her hand and, still grinning, followed her example.

Half an hour later they had tidied the hut, packing as much of their gear as they could. The pigs were enjoying the peelings and Nicholas had refilled the bucket. Maren had made a quick trip to the bushes.

Though less embarrassed than the previous evening, she had found it just as unpleasant and the driving rain had added to her discomfort.

Back in the hut as she folded her waterproof sheet after shaking off the rain, she noticed Nicholas pushing all the ferns into a heap away from the door.

'What are you doing?'

He glanced up. 'Trying to make as much room as possible. We'll have to hold our surgery in here.'

'Why can't we go to their houses?' she asked, wiping her wet face with her towel and smoothing her hair back.

'Mainly because there isn't enough room. But also because their segregated living arrangements make it awkward for me to enter the women's houses and you the men's. I usually see them outside in the hamlet yard, but today –' He gestured at the rain.

Maren crouched beside him as he opened the medical supplies box. 'What do you want me to do?' she asked diffidently. 'I went into research direct from Medical School, so I haven't actually practised medicine.'

'Then it's about time you did. The kinds of medical problems we face can vary considerably. Yaws, scabies and intestinal parasites are common. So is lung disease, acute and chronic. I carry antibiotics for respiratory and gastro-intestinal infections. But most of these casual visits involve treating infected skin conditions, burns, wounds and tropical ulcers from insect bites.'

'Do you keep any records?' Maren helped him to spread his groundsheet then he lifted the medical box onto it.

'I complete the inevitable forms. But that's really for government statistics; keeping track of the drugs used and the conditions treated.'

They washed their hands with an antibacterial liquid detergent, drying them on a sterile towel from a sealed pack.

'Oh yes, I remember, Mr Kanawe's returns in triplicate.' Maren caught Nicholas's eye and they exchanged a knowing smile. In an effort to keep her blossoming happiness under tight control, she retreated behind a mask of professional interest. 'Are personal medical records kept for all the people in this administrative area?'

'In theory,' Nicholas replied. 'It's not easy, though. The villagers are generally more settled now and don't move to new garden sites every few years. But there is still a lot of individual movement between hamlets, villages and even kinship groups, through marriage, illness or family disputes.' He pointed to another sealed packet. 'That contains disposable gloves, and those two are cotton wool and dressings. Adhesive plasters and gauze are in the front section.'

He poured some more disinfectant into a shallow dish. 'You'll find the gloves too big, but that can't be helped. Remember to dip your hands in this –' he put the bowl down and screwed the top back on the bottle '– and change your gloves after every patient with a discharging wound.'

'You're seriously concerned about cross-infection? Out here, in these conditions?' Maren could not hide her incredulity.

Nicholas's gaze was cool. 'Aren't savages entitled

to basic safety precautions, then?'

Maren flinched. 'No,' she stammered, 'I mean – I didn't – you misunderstood me.' She could see a yawning chasm opening up between them. Their fragile friendship, so newly born, was already threatened.

Nicholas sat back on his heels, his face bleak. 'All right, explain.'

'I did *not* mean we shouldn't bother.' She tried to keep her voice calm and even. What she longed to do was to plead with him not to retreat, not to shut her out again. In that instant she realised how much his respect and approval mattered. It shook her. Instinctively she thrust her emotions aside. She must reach him through reason, or she would not reach him at all.

'I was simply expressing my doubts that, given their communal lifestyle and extremely primitive facilities, our precautions could be effective.'

Nicholas studied her for a moment, then picked up the torch and checked the label of each container in the box before passing them over for her to set out on the sheet.

'It would be easy not to bother,' he said then gave a brief self-mocking laugh. 'You wouldn't believe how often I've prescribed a course of antibiotics, with instructions as to how and when they must be taken, and special emphasis on the importance of completing the course. Then I come back a few weeks later and learn the patient either bartered them for trade-store booze, or, after taking a few and beginning to feel better, gave the rest to a relative or friend who probably had something entirely different wrong with them.'

Nicholas closed the box, 'And those are the patients we *can* help. The others –' He broke off, shrugging impatiently, obviously annoyed with himself for revealing his feelings.

Maren sensed he did not want sympathy. 'What others? What about them?'

'You'll see,' Nicholas answered grimly. He got to his feet and went to the doorway. Cupping his hands to his mouth he shouted, then sat down cross-legged on a corner of the groundsheet. 'There's a plastic envelope taped inside the box lid. Inside it you'll find treatment sheets and a ballpoint pen. If you write down the details of each patient as I give them to you it will save a lot of time.'

Maren nodded, took out the pen and papers and put them beside her. 'How do you manage with descriptions of symptoms? I know you speak their language. But does it have words describing illnesses?'

'It can be confusing,' Nicholas admitted. 'As you are already aware there are 700 languages spoken in this country.' He gave her a pointed look, and Maren felt her face grow warm as she recalled the plane journey from Goroka to Okapa. He had infuriated her with his assumption that she knew nothing about the country to which she had come. She had retaliated by delivering a concise summary of the history, geography and demographic status of Papua New Guinea, only to feel gauche and self-conscious when he had mockingly praised her preparation.

'English is the official language,' he said. 'But the scattered Highland groups don't speak it.'

'What do they speak, then?' Maren asked, her self-consciousness fading as her interest grew.

'Tok Pisin. It's a Melanesian pidgin, a language of convenience developed so that early colonists, missionaries and so forth from several European countries could communicate with different tribal groups and each other.'

'You use that here?'

He nodded. 'That and the local Southern Fore dialect, Purosa. It's also reasonably well understood by the Gimi people we'll be visiting later.'

That reminded Maren of something she had been meaning to ask him. 'What about the fighting? What did the men say last night?'

But her question went unanswered as footsteps splashed to a halt outside and a man's voice began a sing-song chant, which rose and fell, ending in a shout.

Maren looked at Nicholas who called out to the man.

'What is it?' she whispered.

Nicholas silenced her with a wave and called again.

The man suddenly leapt into the hut, and Maren caught her breath.

His face was painted white with thick black lines around his eyes and a red stripe down the middle of his forehead and nose. His mouth was a red gash, the colour extending from his lips outward to each ear. He wore an elaborate headdress of beads, shells and plumes. His body was thin and the skin sagged in wrinkles and folds and Maren realised he must be quite old. Several ropes of beads, some shell, some painted seeds, hung from his neck and strands of bark-fibre string were wrapped round his waist and covered his loincloth, falling in bunches front and back.

He struck a menacing pose and barked several phrases at Nicholas who bowed his head and replied evenly. The man chanted again, stamping his feet several times. Then he pointed at Nicholas and turned his face to the roof.

After a few seconds of silence the man waved his hands, jumped in the air, shouted at Nicholas, then with a nod he turned round and walked out.

Maren heard his footsteps splashing away across the yard. She turned to Nicholas. 'What was all that about? Is he the local witch doctor?'

Nicholas shrugged. 'He believes he is. The villagers say he's *long-long*, that's pidgin for dementia or a behavioural peculiarity.'

'But what was it all about?' Maren was bemused.

'He was asking the spirits of his ancestors if I was to be permitted to do my magic here.' He spread his hands, 'They said yes.'

'Do they always say yes?' Maren asked, not sure whether to take him seriously.

'They have so far.'

'What do the other villagers think of him?'

'They tolerate him. He belongs here. He's not violent and he's never harmed anyone. Besides, it's quite possible they believe in what he does.'

'Are you serious?'

Nicholas looked directly at her. 'Haven't you ever crossed your fingers, or touched wood? Ever avoided walking under a ladder, thrown salt over your

118

shoulder? Superstition still has a lot of power in our society. And this country is only just coming out of the Stone Age.'

More footsteps stopped outside and a woman carrying a child peeped shyly round the doorpost.

Nicholas greeted her and coaxed her into the hut. She took a bundle of sweet potatoes from under the woven bark-fibre cape she wore for protection against the rain. It was her only garment except for a short, full skirt of string and several rows of beads. Placing the vegetables beside the door, she glanced uncertainly at Maren who gave her an encouraging smile.

At Nicholas's invitation the woman sat down in the light from the doorway. She pushed the cape back off her shoulders and rested the baby on her crossed legs. Nicholas questioned her.

Sitting out of direct light and slightly apart from both of them, Maren was able to study him without fear of discovery.

His darkly tanned skin, rough-hewn features and thick black hair gave him a fierce, gipsylike appearance, and her heart skipped a beat as she remembered how terrifying he could be when angry. But as she watched him listening carefully to the woman's halting replies, tickling the baby's palm with his index finger, allowing the child to become used to him, she saw a gentleness she had not suspected.

She wondered again at his complexity. This woman and her baby might have been his only patients, so calm and leisurely was his approach. Yet he must know that others would be waiting to see him, some probably without needing to but not wanting to be left out.

He cared deeply about the country and its people. Yet he was equally open about their faults. He was less patronising to them than he was to her.

Yet, despite his dedication, instead of working permanently among the sick he had become a lecturer, teaching a new generation of doctors. That was when he was not trekking through the mountains and forests of this primitive country, following up reports of a disease that was dying out anyway. Why?

Then the child whimpered and Maren switched her gaze as the woman turned him around, pulling aside the piece of grubby cloth in which he was wrapped.

Maren's stomach contracted as she saw that the baby's arm had been burned from shoulder to elbow and yellow streaks on the raw pink flesh showed it was infected.

Nicholas's face registered nothing as he examined the ugly wound carefully, using the torch for extra light. Then he turned to Maren. 'Mix me a one in thirty dilution of Chlorhexidine gluconate solution. Then I'll want – Maren!' His abrupt, incisive use of her name reached her through churning waves of nausea. 'Pull yourself together. You have work to do. Do you hear me?'

She nodded dumbly, swallowing the bitter taste in her throat, feeling her strength return as she took deep breaths. She reached for another enamel bowl and poured in a measure of the concentrated bactericide. Adding the correct amount of distilled water she passed him the bowl with an unopened packet of cotton wool.

'I – I'm sorry,' she whispered as he took them from

her.

'Forget it,' he cut across her stumbling apology, his tone totally impersonal. 'You will assist. Bring that tube of gentamicin cream and the largest burn dressing you can find, then come round to this side of the mother.'

Maren did as she was told. She was about to lift the child's arm when Nicholas's elbow came in front of her like a barrier. 'Gloves,' he said with steely quietness.

Burning with embarrassment at having to be reminded, Maren fumbled a pair from the package behind Nicholas and quickly pushed her hands into them.

'Now, hold the arm steady.'

As he began, with infinite care to bathe the ugly wound, the baby squirmed and whimpered, then began crying in earnest. The woman fidgeted uneasily, glancing from Nicholas to Maren and back to her child.

Nicholas spoke to her, smiling, repeating what he said. The woman nodded, ducking her head shyly before trying to turn the baby's head to her breast. But the child resisted, roaring his unhappiness and pain.

While Maren wondered what she should do to help, Nicholas stripped off his gloves, rested them over the edge of the bowl, then gently but firmly turned the baby's head and held it while the woman placed her nipple in the tiny open mouth.

The noise stopped as the baby responded instinctively and began sucking, making breathless little sobbing sounds in his throat.

Nicholas pulled his gloves on again, and with another word to the woman who started crooning to her child, he resumed his task.

Within 15 minutes the arm had been thoroughly cleansed, dried, the antibiotic cream applied and the dressing bandaged in place. The woman pulled her cape round herself and the baby and, smiling her thanks, stepped out of the hut, the baby nestled sleepily against her, still contentedly sucking.

Now they were alone once more, Maren waited for Nicholas to give her the tongue-lashing she knew she deserved. She was sure the only reason he had treated her momentary weakness with such restraint was his reluctance to further upset the mother or baby. But now he could let fly.

That she had no experience of accident and emergency cases was no excuse. Nor could she expect him to understand that while she had really enjoyed her physiology training, absorbing like a sponge the theory of chemical and physical processes involved in the functioning of a living organism, contact with sick people and observing operations had been too harrowing.

She had found it impossible to think of patients as "the Hodgkin's sarcoma", or "the diabetic gangrene". She had wasted valuable time and incurred the wrath of her tutors on frequent occasions because of her inability to limit her attention to the site of the disease and ignore the fact that it was part of a living person who was anxious and in pain. It had been worse with children. They were so small, so helpless.

How ironic it was that Nicholas should have accused her of being cold and uncaring in her attitude when he had been describing kuru to her. The truth was that she had turned to research instead of practical medicine because she had cared too much.

Why didn't he say something? She wished he would get it over and done with. While nothing was said it raised another barrier between them, another opportunity for misunderstanding. God knew there were enough of those already. If he was not going to mention it then she would have to.

'Right, take the details down before the next one arrives.' He gathered up the soiled cotton wool and torn dressing packet, tossing them into a paper sack.

Maren hesitated, 'But – aren't you –'

'I've told you what to do,' he interrupted. 'Do it.' He stripped off his gloves and threw them in after.

Maren scrambled back to her sleeping bag and picked up the pen and forms. 'Yes, I know, but –'

Nicholas cut across her again, 'Name Akeku, age, 12 months. Diagnosis – what's the matter? Do you need the torch or am I going too fast?'

'Neither,' she said hastily, 'I just wanted –'

'For God's sake, woman,' he exploded. 'Will you get on with it? You are meant to be saving time, not wasting it.'

'Will you listen to me,' Maren cried. 'I am trying to explain.'

'And I am not interested,' Nicholas retorted sharply. 'If you want to indulge in an orgy of breast-beating and self-pity, do it in your own time. Now, have you got the child's name and age?'

'Yes,' Maren answered tight-lipped and furious. Who did he think he was? All she had wanted was to apologise, explain why she had reacted that way.

123

What had he meant by that crack about self-pity? Just because the sight of people in pain upset her …

Maren was suddenly very still. *Her*, it upset *her*. She had been more concerned with the effect on her than with the feelings of the patients. Even while she was professing to care too much, it was *her* feelings that had counted most, upon which she had acted. She brushed her hand across her face, deeply shaken by the flash of insight. He had known. Nicholas Calder had known.

'Right,' he said, breaking into her thoughts. 'Describe the injury.' Still immersed in her shattering discovery, she tried to gather her scattered wits.

'You heard me. I suppose you did notice it? Or were you sitting there with your eyes shut.' His sarcasm bit deep. 'The injury?' he repeated, raising one eyebrow as he tapped his fingers on his knee with growing impatience.

'A second-degree thermal burn on the right upper arm,' she replied through clenched teeth.

He continued to tap. 'And?'

She stared back at him, not understanding, then it clicked. 'With secondary infection,' she added.

'Fill in the rest of that line, and add the treatment.' He turned away.

'Am I permitted a question?' She nearly added 'sir', but decided against it and was glad she had resisted the impulse when he turned his cold gaze onto her.

'Provided it concerns the patient we've just seen.'

'It does,' she snapped. He was so arrogant, so sure of himself. 'If you are so anxious to save time why did you use gentamicin? There's triclocarban and povidone-iodine in the box. Both are suitable for burns and need fewer applications.'

Nicholas studied her for a moment, 'If you had looked closely at the burn you would have seen that in certain places it was oozing serum.' His voice was expressionless. 'If you had examined the container labels properly, you would have seen that both the triclocarban and povidone-iodine are in ointment form and so not suitable for moist lesions.'

Maren's anger collapsed like a pricked balloon as he continued. 'Without laboratory tests, which are obviously impossible to obtain here, I can't be sure which pathogens have caused the infection nor how sensitive they may or may not be to antibiotics. Gentamicin has the widest range and degree of antibacterial activity and when used topically is relatively is free from side-effects. In the case of a child that's rather important, don't you think?'

Cold contempt had crept into his voice which he made no attempt to hide. Maren knew that its presence was entirely her own fault. Her reckless behaviour had not only made her look a complete fool, it had wrecked their budding friendship. What was it that drove her headlong into these confrontations with him? What was she trying to prove?

The last two days had turned her whole life upside down. Beliefs she had held about herself, her work, her relationships with other people, beliefs that had seemed so firm, so right, were crumbling, blown like dust in the wind.

'I'll check the dressing this afternoon and leave cream and fresh dressings for the mother to apply.'

His voice was once more expressionless. 'There doesn't seem to be any damage to underlying tissue – ' he paused, frowning '– but that infection will delay healing.' He eyed her briefly. 'Add a note asking Okapa to follow up on it as soon as possible.'

Maren nodded. On the surface nothing had changed. He was discussing treatment as he would have with any colleague. But something had gone. Something that had been there and now was missing, and she grieved for it.

More footsteps splashed outside and another face, this time a man's, appeared in the doorway. Nicholas greeted him and beckoned him inside.

The man tossed a bundle of sugarcane onto the sweet potatoes then squatted in front of Nicholas. With suspicious glances at Maren he began a long, complaining description of his symptoms, clutching his stomach and contorting his face so they were left in no doubt as to his sufferings. As he talked he scratched the soles of his feet.

Maren couldn't help wondering if the man was exaggerating. But Nicholas treated him with the same patience he had shown the mother, asking questions while he tapped the man's chest and back then listened with his stethoscope.

He turned to Maren. 'Pour some of your Perrier water into that measure.' He pointed to a small polythene beaker with graduated marks on the side.

Maren did as he asked, wondering if he was going to pretend it was medicine. It was hardly ethical, but she had read enough psychology to know that if a person really believed that the medicine they were about to swallow would stop their stomach ache or back pains, then often it did. It wasn't entirely a case of "mind over matter" – recent research had shown it had something to do with the brain triggering the release of endorphins, the body's own pain-relieving substances.

But when Nicholas gave the man the water, she noticed he also gave him a pink tablet taken from a blister pack of six. Nicholas was taking the vivid description of symptoms seriously.

After the man had gone, taking the remaining tablets with him, Nicholas looked round. 'Ready?' Maren nodded. 'Name Ebote, age 40, diagnosis –' He stopped. 'Give me your opinion. There is a certain amount of bronchial and lung inflammation, and he is complaining of nausea, colicky pains and diarrhoea.'

Maren's mind raced. 'He seemed rather thin. Is he also anaemic?' As Nicholas nodded she went through the signs and symptoms once more in her head, trying to remember something else she had noticed, something that gave another clue. She closed her eyes and pictured the man, squatting in front of Nicholas, shuffling his feet as he scratched first one then the other. That was it. That was what she had been trying to remember.

'Hookworm?' She held her breath as she waited for his reaction. He had told her that intestinal parasites were common out here and hookworm was a particularly unpleasant infection. The larvae entered the body through bare skin, usually of the feet, working their way into the lungs, then up the windpipe to be swallowed. When they reached the intestines they attached themselves to the wall of the gut and existed by sucking blood.

Nicholas nodded. 'Fill in the form. The treatment is 100 milligrammes of Mebendazole twice daily for three days. That will clear his system. But with the high risk of re-infestation he'll probably need another treatment when the regular medics come through.'

Maren was momentarily disappointed. Then common-sense reasserted itself. His matter-of-fact acceptance of her diagnosis was, in its way, a compliment. And had he expressed surprise she would probably have accused him of sarcasm or patronage.

During the next hour Nicholas treated a boy for a septic foot cut on a stone, an older woman's ulcerated leg, and a little girl of three with bronchitis. She had cowered behind her mother, her brown eyes huge and fear-filled as Nicholas coaxed her into letting him listen to her chest.

When the little girl had gone and no one else had taken her place, Maren assumed that surgery was over. But just as she was about to ask Nicholas, who had pulled a folder from his pack and was studying the typed papers inside it, the girl who had brought their food the previous evening stepped into the hut.

She spoke softly to Nicholas, fidgeting shyly, peeping at him through lowered lashes. He nodded and she turned to help a woman into the hut.

As the woman stumbled in, clumsy and erratic, Maren recognised her as the lone figure she'd seen returning from the gardens the previous evening. She still clasped the same stick and her legs and arms trembled so violently she would have fallen if Nicholas had not got up quickly and held her. Freed, the girl flashed him a coquettish smile, sauntered over to the door, and plonked herself down.

'Come over here,' Nicholas ordered Maren. She put down the pen and forms. 'Take my place. Hold her under the elbow. Her name is Tigi. She's the girl's mother.'

Maren darted a quick look at the girl who seemed unconcerned, looking round the hut and craning to see what was laid out on the sheet and in the medical box.

Maren took Tigi's arm, noticing the woman's mouth was fixed in a dull grin.

'I'm going to ask her to do various movements to test the progress of the disease,' Nicholas said, then spoke to Tigi. Her reply was slow and slurred.

Responding to Nicholas's directions, Maren shifted her grip to hold Tigi round the waist as he took away the stick. Tigi sagged against Maren as she tried with slow, painful effort to touch the tips of her index fingers together. But despite her desperate concentration the fingers passed each other several inches apart.

Next, she tried to lift one foot off the ground with her eyes closed. At once she staggered and would have fallen had Maren not grabbed her.

Nicholas moved round behind them and clapped his hands. Tigi's arms and legs jerked wildly, became stiff, then twitched uncontrollably while her hands and fingers writhed in slow, twisting, snakelike movements.

'Nicholas, she's slipping. I can't hold her,' Maren cried anxiously and at once his arms shot out to catch Tigi as she lurched out of Maren's grasp.

He dropped the stick and lowered Tigi gently to

the floor where she sat, shivering and trembling, her head jerking unceasingly in a sideways nod.

Maren returned to her place and sat down. 'Do you want me to fill in a treatment form?'

'No,' Nicholas replied abruptly, then picked up the folder and scribbled a few notes.

Without warning Tigi started to laugh. The sound was eerie and sent shivers down Maren's spine as it went on and on, until she wanted to shake the trembling woman and shout at her to stop.

She looked at Nicholas who tossed the folder aside. 'This is kuru?'

He nodded and began repacking the medical box.

Maren looked once more at Tigi. Her face was still contorted in a ghastly grin. Though the horrifying laughter had diminished, she still giggled every few moments. Fighting down the unease the woman's behaviour roused in her, Maren was suddenly overcome by a profound sense of pity. 'How old is she?'

'She's 32,' Nicholas answered flatly.

'How long –' Maren faltered.

'She's in second stage now. She could last another nine months. Or it could be as little as three.'

'What – what will happen next?'

'She'll be unable to sit up, the tremors and speech defect will become more severe. She will become totally incontinent and deep bedsores will develop. Her swallowing reflex will fail and she'll be unable to eat or drink. Finally hypostatic pneumonia will develop and she'll die.'

He turned away and spoke to the girl who crouched down beside her mother, tied a rain cape over her and with Nicholas's help got Tigi onto her feet. Clinging to her stick with one hand and her daughter with the other, Tigi stumbled painfully out of the hut.

Maren was shocked as Nicholas began to clear up.

'What are you doing?'

'What does it look like?' he retorted.

'But – Tigi – you sent her away. Aren't you going to give her anything?'

'What do you suggest?' His voice was growing colder and harder with each reply.

Maren was too agitated to notice. She shrugged helplessly. 'I don't know, but surely there must be something you could do?'

'If there was, don't you think I'd have done it?' he snarled, then bolted to his feet and went to the door. He paused, raking a hand through his hair.

Staring at his broad shoulders and bent head as he slowly rubbed the back of his neck, Maren realised his anger was really frustration at being powerless in the face of the nightmarish disease that was destroying Tigi.

'The rain is stopping,' he growled over his shoulder as he picked up the bucket then strode outside to empty it over the fence.

Maren looked out at the sky. The heavy blanket of cloud was breaking up, showing patches of blue that grew larger as the sun burned away the cloud and glistened in the puddles scattered across the hamlet yard.

The villagers were emerging from their houses. Men and women built fires with wood kept dry by bark-fibre shelters. Children played, chasing one another through the puddles. A girl comforted a crying baby then gave it to her mother to nurse.

The woman with the ulcerated leg dragged a mat woven from flattened pit-pit stalks out to a fire and sat down. Taking vegetables from a net bag she peeled them then stuffed them into bamboo cooking cylinders.

Two boys were making a trap while a man tied kunai grass into bundles for thatching.

Talk and laughter filled the clean damp air which was growing warmer every second.

'When are we leaving?' Maren asked Nicholas as he re-entered the hut.

'First thing in the morning.'

'Which of the boys will be going with us?'

'Boys?' he sounded surprised. 'What for?'

'To build fires, do the cooking, collect food–'

Nicholas laughed aloud. 'Why on earth should I take a boy when I've got you?'

'Me?' Maren's eyes widened. 'But I'm not – I've never – Is this another of your jokes?'

Nicholas shook his head with slow deliberation, his eyes dancing.

'Forget it,' Maren said flatly. 'I'm a doctor, not a skivvy. I'm here for research purposes, not to win a Girlguiding badge for camp craft.'

Nicholas moved lazily across to tower over her, a smile playing round his mouth. As she met his gaze, Maren's stomach quaked.

'Let's get something straight, once and for all.' His voice was very soft and gooseflesh broke out on Maren's arms. 'You are here on my say-so. Not one word,' he warned as she opened her mouth to protest.

'No favours you said. Remember? You would pull your weight? Well that is exactly what you are going to do.'

'And if I refuse?' She hadn't intended to say it, but it was so maddening, the way he always twisted the things she'd said to get his own way.

'I'll leave you here and go on alone.'

'You wouldn't dare,' Maren stormed. 'Professor Brent –'

He didn't even let her finish. 'Try me,' he coaxed and it was crystal clear he wasn't bluffing.

Chapter Eight

After a late lunch they had spent the remainder of the day apart. Maren washed her shirt and a pair of socks, hanging them on the fence to dry while she studied the file Bilas Kanawe had given her. It had made sobering reading. There was no doubt that the malaria problem was getting worse. The disease was beginning to appear in villages previously unaffected. It was also increasing among people already taking preventative doses of antimalarial drugs. As she turned the pages Maren realised how vital it was that she obtain blood samples from a newly infected first-time sufferer, and specimens of eggs, larvae and adult mosquitoes. For it was possible that the detailed examination using powerful electron microscopes, together with various chemical tests, would reveal the changes in the malaria parasite which made it resistant to drugs.

The hamlet had been virtually deserted during the afternoon as the women, their children and the older girls, had gone to the gardens to work and collect food for the evening meal.

Nicholas had gone fishing with some of the men in a river about a mile away down the far side of the ridge. They had brought back a dozen large fish and when the women returned from the gardens only minutes after the men, preparations for a feast began at once.

While the women peeled, cut and tied vegetables into bundles, men laid the fire on which the cooking stones were to be heated. Two boys cleaned rubbish and water from the cooking pit while several others who had been trapping in the forest brought back half a dozen rats and frogs which they skinned and gutted, lighting a small fire of their own on which to cook.

When the fire had burned down the men pushed the hot stones into the cooking pit with long sticks. Special leaves were then laid on the stones, and the fish and bunches of vegetables were placed on these.

Once the pit was full, banana leaves were laid on the food and covered with earth to hold in the heat. Then water, brought from the spring in long bamboo containers, was poured into the pit through gaps left in the dirt cap, and the food was left to cook in the steam.

Maren had been watching the preparations from the hut when Nicholas walked in and dropped a bulging net bag down beside her.

'What's this?' she asked in surprise.

'Fruit for the journey: wild mango, passion fruit and lemons,' he replied. Then, collecting soap and a towel, he walked out again before she could say anything, pausing only to call over his shoulder, 'The hut's yours. I shan't be back till late.'

Not wishing to waste the guaranteed privacy, Maren took the bucket down to the spring. He was there, several yards down the slope, stripped to the waist, cupping handfuls of water over his face and neck. He did not acknowledge her presence. Not sure whether it was deliberate or simply that he had not seen her, Maren filled the bucket quickly and returned to the hut.

All the way back it plagued her. Should she have said something? Should she have tried to bridge the gap that once again yawned so widely between them?

She cursed her shyness. She had never found it easy to start conversations. Remarks about the weather seemed so trite. Though she'd heard guests at her sister's weekend parties turn on sparkling wit or profundity like a tap, Maren knew it wasn't her. She had tried it once and had sounded so brittle and artificial it had made her cringe inside.

Anyway, how did you chat to someone who obviously wasn't in the mood to chat back? If you and that person were not on good terms to start with, it was even more difficult.

Maren felt better after her bath. Dressed once again, with a light sweater over her shirt to keep out the evening chill, she brushed her hair thoroughly and left it loose on her shoulders. Then she took the bucket out to the fence and emptied it.

The men were opening the cooking pit, spurred on by shouts and laughter from the rest of the villagers grouped round two large fires. Maren paused to watch as men distributed the steaming food to waiting relatives and friends. The women further divided it into portions for the children who gathered in groups of their own age and sex to talk together while they ate.

Nicholas sat with the older men, talking and laughing with them. He looked up, smiling his thanks as Tigi's daughter took him banana leaves piled with cooked fish and vegetables. He did not even glance in Maren's direction, apparently totally absorbed in what the man on his left was saying.

He had abandoned her, awkward and out of place among strangers whose language she did not speak, while he enjoyed himself, obviously quite at home.

Maren tried to stir up some indignation at his rudeness. Instead she began to feel sorry for herself. But the memory of his scathing anger and his accusation of self-indulgence made earlier that morning flashed through her mind. Instantly she shied away from both the memory and the emotion that had provoked it and concentrated on the villagers.

Tigi's daughter left the group once more. This time the girl was coming towards her, bringing food. Maren dropped the bucket inside the hut and accepted the banana leaves, thanking the girl who dimpled and, tilting her head on one side, asked Maren a question.

Maren shrugged helplessly. 'I'm sorry, I don't understand.' The girl touched Maren's arm and pointed towards the seated groups. Maren hesitated. She did not want to intrude, aware that she could contribute nothing to the conversation. Nor, she realised, did she want to sit alone in the hut to eat her meal.

The girl tugged again and this time Maren went with her. She sat on the edge of the group, grateful for the illusion of being included. Her face ached from returning the smiles of the women and girls who kept glancing at her, then turning to whisper and giggle between themselves.

The fish was delicious and she enjoyed the hot

sweet potato, kumu, pit-pit and mushrooms.

When everyone had eaten their fill, and night had fallen with the suddenness that always surprises visitors to the tropics, more branches were thrown on the fires.

Children dozed in their mothers' laps as the reedy sound of a flute rose into the night sky. Another one joined in. Then drums, deep-toned and resonant, added a rhythm that stirred something deep inside her.

The men began to chant. The women took up the song, clapping their hands to the beat. Back and forth it flew between them.

Maren hugged her knees as she stared into the flames, feeling the alien music seeping into her, moving her with its powerful rhythms. The song ended and another began, a slow, haunting tune played by two flutes in harmony.

As she listened Maren was suddenly overwhelmed by loneliness. In the past she had known odd days when she had been aware of a yearning, a need for something more. She had ignored it, plunging herself into work or study, refusing to acknowledge what she saw as a weakness.

But tonight there was no work with which to smother the feeling. She had finished reading the file and could remember most of its contents. She would find no escape there. Nor had she any other books to distract her. As the plaintive music washed over her, touching an answering chord in her heart, Maren slipped quietly away from the group, aware of not belonging with them. But as she looked up at the black night sky she had no idea where she did belong.

She slowly crossed the hamlet yard on the edge of the glow, where firelight merged into darkness, seeking Nicholas. Finding him, she drank in the sight.

His long legs were crossed in front of him, elbows resting on his knees, fingers linked. He looked completely relaxed. His shirt was open at the neck, the sleeves rolled up, and his dark skin gleamed in the flickering light. The dancing flames cast shadows across his face so that his eyes seemed deeper, his cheekbones higher.

He turned his head very slightly, seeming to stare right at her. She could not move, held immobile by the sheer force of his personality. The nameless yearning welled up in her once more. Then slowly, casually, he turned away.

She bent her head and her hair fell forward, hiding her face as it burned with the turbulence inside her. Pushing her hands into her pockets she walked slowly back to the hut.

Sometime later, lying awake in the darkness, she heard Nicholas return then the scrape and rustle of the door being pushed into place. He did not speak and neither did she. But with a sigh that released her from the shackles of unsuspected tension, she turned over and immediately fell asleep.

The next morning he shook her awake, releasing her shoulder and moving away the instant her eyes opened. After dressing and washing, she ate a quick breakfast of mango, banana and a small piece of honeycomb, a gift from the mother of the bronchitic child, while Nicholas carried his rucksack and the medical box up to the Land Rover. He accepted without comment her insistence on carrying her own rucksack. He rolled and tied both sleeping bags in their groundsheets and scooped up the net bag containing the fruit, to which had been added raw and cooked sweet potato, cobs of corn and a bunch of pit-pit stalks.

On reaching the top of the steep, muddy path, Maren took a last look down onto the little hamlet. The villagers were beginning to stir. A baby cried. Down from their roost, chickens squawked and pecked in the dirt and the pigs squealed as they gathered, jostling and shoving, outside the fence.

'Come on,' Nicholas shouted impatiently, starting the engine, and it was with mixed feelings that she turned her back on the hamlet and hurried to climb into the Land Rover.

They left just after dawn. Mist shrouded the mountains and the trees dripped condensation in the early morning chill. The coughing roar of the engine shattered the stillness, sending green pigeons and black cockatoos flapping with startled cries into the gloom of the surrounding forest.

The track was full of puddles and water-filled ruts and the wheels churned the surface to liquid mud. Nicholas drove with frowning concentration, trying to avoid the biggest ones. But the track was so narrow he rarely succeeded. Maren clung to the seat with one hand and the door with the other, while the muscles in Nicholas's arms stood out like knotted rope as he guided the vehicle over the potholes.

They were both thrown about by the bumps and jolts, picking up speed on the drier stretches, only to slow to a crawl as they hit yet another patch of rutted mud and puddles. The engine's deafening roar made conversation impossible. The hours ticked by. The sun climbed higher in the azure sky, heating the air inside the vehicle until both were blistered with perspiration and breathing was an effort.

Maren looked ahead to the forested peaks as she wiped her face and neck. Then she glanced sideways and felt a twinge of unease as she saw that the edge of the track fell steeply away, a tumble of earth, stones and mud showing where it had recently collapsed. What remained looked horrifyingly narrow. There were cracks and gullies criss-crossing the track and she guessed that water had caused the subsidence.

She darted a glance at Nicholas, her unease flaring into real alarm as he edged the vehicle closer. Maren's knuckles gleamed white as she gripped the seat, biting her lip to stop herself warning him to be careful. He knew what he was doing. He had probably used this track a dozen times and she would not increase her popularity by bothering him with statements of the obvious while he was trying to work out the best way of dealing with the situation.

He stopped the Land Rover a yard from the first deep crack. 'I'm going to have a look,' he said. 'Stay there.' He squeezed himself between the vehicle and the wall of earth and rock through which the track had been cut, and walked forward to examine the ground, crouching to study the edges of a wide crack.

Maren gazed at his back. She wished she could do something, anything. She felt so useless just sitting there. It wasn't as if she could see very much. The windscreen was splattered with mud and dead insects, and the screens at the side windows limited the view. She would just have to be patient. If he wanted help he would not hesitate to demand it. Meanwhile the best thing she could do was keep out of his way, and keep quiet.

She sat back in her seat and felt the Land Rover shift. Dismissing it as the echo of her own movement she wondered what Nicholas was planning to do.

There was another small jolt. Then slowly, so slowly that at first she was sure she was imagining it, the Land Rover started to tilt sideways and backwards.

For a moment she was frozen into petrified silence. The movement halted. Almost too frightened to utter a sound in case that should provoke it to start again, Maren called Nicholas's name. Fear had dried her throat and the sound emerged as a cracked whisper. He did not hear it.

With a slow, sickening lurch the back of the vehicle slewed round, sank a few inches, and stopped again.

Maren was pressed against her door where the first movement had tipped her. Glancing out of the window she could no longer see the edge of the track, only the drop which seemed to be rushing up to meet her. She shut her eyes tightly.

Sweat trickled down her back, soaking her shirt as she forced them open again. Nicholas still had his back to her. But, as she watched, he stood up and turned towards the Land Rover.

Her perception heightened by terror, she watched the blood drain out of his face leaving it ashen beneath his tan. Then, as if in slow motion, she saw him hurl himself forward, his arm outstretched to grab the driver's door.

'No, don't!' she screamed, certain that any sudden movement would send the Land Rover with her inside it toppling over the edge.

He skidded to a halt only inches away and Maren watched conscious thought override automatic reaction. He edged closer and squeezed through the gap between the wall and vehicle. With infinite care he pulled open the door. 'You must come across to this side,' he said.

Maren did not dare turn her head to look at him. She moistened her parched lips with her tongue. 'I'm scared to move.' It emerged as a husky whisper. 'What if –'

'Listen to me,' Nicholas interrupted. He sounded perfectly calm. 'Your weight on that side could tip the whole thing over. You must move across.' The tension round his eyes and mouth and the sweat beading his forehead and upper lip belied his cool control. 'Lean towards me. Slowly now.' With the door resting on his back, he reached in to her, careful not to touch anything.

Maren began to inch along the seat. Metal groaned and creaked. She threw herself flat, rigid with fear, her eyes shut tight. The Land Rover lurched again and sank a few inches more. She stopped breathing.

'Come on, Maren.' Nicholas's voice was raw with urgency. 'Easy now, take my hand.'

She raised her head and slowly reached out towards him. His fingers touched hers, brushed her palm then grasped her wrist. He began to pull her steadily upwards across the seats.

Her foot caught on the transmission tunnel and wedged behind the gear lever. 'Wait,' she called hoarsely. 'I'm stuck.' The adrenalin of fear surged through her, making her heart hammer. Blood pounded in her ears. Carefully she worked her foot free and started moving once more.

Reaching the driver's seat, she eased herself upright, sliding one leg then the other over the door sill.

Nicholas edged backwards still holding her wrist tightly. 'Put your weight onto your feet. Slowly.'

Fighting an overwhelming urge to scramble free as fast as she could, Maren leaned forward. Nicholas took her other hand, her bottom slid off the seat and she was out.

He pushed her along the side of the Land Rover. Then lifting the door off his back he allowed it to close very gently. They were both clear.

'Oh,' Maren murmured, and began to shake. 'I – I th –think I –' She swayed and Nicholas released her hands and caught her round the waist, holding her close.

'It's all right,' he reassured. 'It's OK. You're safe now.'

Maren leaned gratefully against him as waves of dizziness rolled over her. To think that only ten minutes ago she had been bored. 'S – s –sorry,' she mumbled against his chest as she clung to his shirt, her teeth chattering uncontrollably, 'I – I f – feel such a f – fool.'

She could hear his steady heartbeat and his arms were warm and strong and so comforting. He laughed and the sound vibrated deep in his chest. 'You're entitled to a case of the shakes. My knees bear a strong resemblance to jelly right now.'

Maren tilted her head back to look up at him. 'You don't have to pretend just to save my pride,' she said with a wry smile. 'I've never been so frightened in my life and I don't care who knows it.'

'Who's pretending?' Nicholas grimaced. 'You don't think I make a habit of this, do you?'

Maren felt her eyes widen. 'You mean – this is the first time … You've never –'

He shook his head.

'But you were so calm. You knew exactly what to do.'

He shrugged. 'Out here you learn to think on your feet. In any case, one of us panicking was enough. As you were stuck in there, you had first claim.'

The ground had stopped heaving beneath Maren's feet and she could feel her strength returning. Reaction that had made her feel sick and lightheaded was fading, helped by Nicholas's laconic attitude towards the incident.

But as shock wore off, so awareness grew. For a few minutes he had represented nothing more than a lifeline, a source of strength and comfort. But now the immediate danger was past, she was once more vividly alive to his effect on her as a man. His arms tightened and she knew that for him too something had changed.

They were both very still. Maren could hear her own pulse, its quickening beat nothing to do with fear.

Nicholas's cheek rested lightly against her hair and his warm breath caressed her face.

The moment lingered, an oasis of peace amid the stress and activity of the past few days. Then his hands gripped her shoulders and he moved her away, startling her with the sudden, forceful movement.

He stared at her, a deep frown creasing his forehead and narrowing his eyes. But for an instant Maren glimpsed uncertainty in his dark gaze, an unguarded vulnerability that astonished and touched her.

Her smile was wry and hesitant. 'Time to get the show on the road again?'

He did not respond at once, as if his thoughts were elsewhere. Then his expression cleared and he released her with the flicker of an answering smile.

As she watched him edge round the back of the Land Rover she could still feel the pressure of his strong fingers.

'Sure you're OK?' He tossed the question over his shoulder, cool and casual, once more in command of himself and the situation. But for a fleeting instant Maren had seen beneath the mask. And what she had seen changed everything.

She nodded. 'I'm fine, really.' She followed him.

'That's good, because you are about to prove just how serious you were. Doing your bit? Pulling your weight?' He eyed her critically, 'Not that you've got much to pull.'

'At five foot ten and over nine-and-a-half stone I'm hardly a sylph,' she retorted.

'How much over?' He was openly sceptical.

'Well, maybe not all that much,' she admitted. 'But I wish you'd stop judging me on my appearance.'

Their eyes met, hers defiant, his speculative, both aware of the wider implications of her heartfelt request.

'All right.' He nodded slowly. Then, as she tried to pass him, his arm shot out, barring her way. 'Hang on a minute. Sylph or not, if you start dancing about on the edge it will reduce our chances of saving the Land Rover and our baggage.'

Maren stepped back hastily. 'Sorry,' she muttered, flustered. But Nicholas had already turned away and was walking back down the track, keeping well away from the edge, scanning the forest and undergrowth on the lower side. Then he jumped down and began making his way back towards Maren, examining the edge of the crude dirt road.

'Come on down here,' he shouted, waving an arm. 'Look,' he pointed as Maren scrambled after him, fighting her way through the tangle of ferns, shrubs and thorn bushes that tore at her clothes. 'The bit giving way is only about ten feet long.'

Only ten feet? She said nothing.

'Before we make any attempt to move the Land Rover we'll have to shore that stretch up.'

'How?'

'Ever wanted to be a lumberjack?' Nicholas asked by way of an answer.

'I can't say it was high on my list of possible careers.'

'Well, you're about to try it.'

'Terrific.' Maren pulled a face. 'I suppose you just happen to have a chainsaw in the toolkit?'

'Not exactly. Wait there.' Retracing his steps Nicholas heaved himself up onto the track and disappeared. He returned a couple of minutes later with a large axe and a machete that he handed to

147

Maren. 'Stay behind me, out of the way.'

'What's the plan?' she asked.

'See those?' He pointed to two tall thick trees standing about eight feet apart just below the level of the track. 'I'm going to drop this one –' he tapped the trunk of a sturdy evergreen '– to fall across the front of those two. It should prevent the edge of the track collapsing any further.'

'What do you want me to do?'

'Cut small shrubs and palm or fern fronds and spread them between the track edge and the trees. They should provide enough packing to hold the earth in place. Whatever you do, don't move in front of me. If this tree twists as it falls the base could kick out sideways. If that happens ...' He left the sentence unfinished but Maren's imagination completed the picture. 'And for God's sake watch what you're doing with that machete, it has an edge like a scalpel.'

Clenching her teeth to hold back an acid retort, Maren turned to begin hacking at the undergrowth. It was harder than she expected. Tendrils of creeper coiled round fronds, branches, stems and leaves, effectively tying everything together like a huge, three-dimensional web.

A rhythmic "thunk" echoed through the forest and she glanced over her shoulder to see Nicholas swinging the axe in a flat arc to bite into the trunk at exactly the same spot with each slow, almost lazy, strike.

Maren watched him for a moment, seeing how easily he balanced on the sloping ground, one long leg slightly above the other. His heavily muscled shoulders threatened to split his shirt as he swung the axe back, then let it fly at the trunk, using the weight of the metal head to add force and momentum to each blow.

She turned quickly back to her task, bending and slashing, then tugging the reluctant fronds free and tossing them onto a pile. When she had a large armful she dropped the heavy, broad-bladed knife, edged her way up the incline and threw the vegetation just below the track edge.

A short while later, arms aching, hands red and sore, one from grasping and pulling the foliage, the other rubbed by the wooden handle of the machete, she was about to throw her third load when Nicholas shouted.

'There she goes!'

Mindful of his warning, Maren stumbled backwards, caught her foot in a root, and landed with a jarring thump on her bottom.

She saw Nicholas leap sideways as, with a cracking, splintering groan the tree slowly swayed, then began to topple, crashing exactly where he had predicted.

He glanced round. Maren was just scrambling to her feet. 'What are you doing down there?' he demanded.

'I got tired. I was taking a rest,' she retorted, as she brushed earth, leaves and bits of broken twig from her back and legs.

His eyes glinted dangerously. But he could not entirely hide the grin that lifted the corners of his mouth. 'Well, when you're ready, perhaps you'll finish plugging any gaps under that trunk. But do it from the lower side,' he reminded her.

Maren gathered up the foliage she had dropped. The fronds and branches scratched her hands and arms and caught on her shirt and trousers. When she had finished she climbed back up to where Nicholas was standing over a sapling he had just felled.

'What's that for?' she asked.

'A lever.' With several swift blows he severed the top third of the sapling, leaving a pole as thick as his forearm, and roughly eight feet long. 'I can't use the jack, the ground is too soft,' he explained, lifting the sapling and jamming it under the back end of the Land Rover. 'But this should stop it sinking any deeper while you clear the mud away from round the wheel.'

'While I what?'

'You heard me. Get moving.' He turned his attention to working the sapling under the vehicle.

Maren retrieved the machete and scrambled up the incline to where the Land Rover was tilting ominously over the edge of the track. The back wheel was trapped in oozing mud that reached almost to the top of the tyre.

She reached in with the machete, trying to use it as a spade. But the broad flat blade was too awkward and cumbersome. With a weary sigh she tossed it aside. Resting one hip on the incline she reached under the sapling which creaked as Nicholas forced it further under the vehicle, plunged her hand into the soft, stinking mud and began scooping it out from around the wheel.

It was hard, filthy, back-breaking work. Every muscle protested at the awkward position she was forced to adopt. Perspiration trickled down her back and between her breasts, sticking her shirt to her skin. It dribbled down her temples and into her eyes. She had to keep wiping her face on her sleeve.

The Land Rover groaned and would have sunk further into the mud had the sapling not halted its downward tilt. Maren hardly dared to breathe as the vehicle settled on the slim trunk. Suddenly realising that she was directly in its path should the sapling break, she rolled out of the way, heedless of the mud and debris smearing her clothes.

She looked up to see Nicholas towering over her, his arms full of small branches and twigs. 'You do seem to lie around a lot,' he observed.

Maren glared at him as she struggled to her feet. She had never been so thirsty in her life. Her tongue felt like a strip of leather and her throat was parched.

Nicholas moved past her and knelt to pack the vegetation around the wheel, jamming it down hard under the tyre.

'What now?' she asked wearily as he stood up again.

'You see where the pole sticks out over the tree-trunk? I want you to go and press down with all your strength on that end. It should stop the Land Rover tilting any further over while I try and drive it back onto the track.'

Maren looked at the pole, at the Land Rover and then at Nicholas. 'It won't work,' she announced, wiping the mud off her hands and arms with a bunch of leaves.

He frowned. 'Of course it will.'

'It won't. The idea is fine,' she said before he could interrupt. 'But it won't work that way around.

151

You said yourself I don't have much weight. Well neither am I strong enough to hold the Land Rover up on that pole, never mind levering it out. We'll have to swap jobs.'

She saw by his expression that he recognised the truth in her statement. But he wasn't happy with her suggestion.

'There isn't any alternative,' she insisted. He was probably finding it hard to accept that she was right and he hadn't thought of it first.

'Have you ever driven one of these before?' Nicholas demanded.

'Of course,' she lied. 'My sister has one. They use it the farm.' That part was true at least. She had often sat beside Lucy on drives round the estate. It couldn't be all that different from driving an ordinary car. She waited, giving him what she hoped was a confident smile.

'OK,' he decided. 'But for God's sake, be careful.'

'Don't worry.' Her tone was tart. 'I won't damage your precious vehicle.' She pushed past him, about to clamber up onto the track. But Nicholas seized her arm and roughly pulled her back.

'It's not the Land Rover I'm worried about,' he growled.

For one long, heart-stopping moment they stared at each other. Then he released her arm and gave her a gentle push. 'Go on up, I'll follow. I want to be sure you know what you're doing.'

Maren did not react to the jibe, still stunned by what he had said. But there was no time to consider what it signified.

'Now,' he said as they looked in at the controls

through the driver's window, 'it's not that I doubt your expertise.' Maren knew that meant he did. But she kept quiet and concentrated on the extra knobs and levers. How she wished she had taken more interest in his driving on the way up here. She prayed she would be able to remember his instructions.

'When you've started the engine, pull the red lever to engage the lower gear ratio and automatic four-wheel drive. Don't change out of first gear. That way you'll have maximum grip and should avoid wheelspin. OK?'

Maren nodded, biting the inside of her lower lip. Why hadn't she kept her mouth shut? Why hadn't she simply done as he'd wanted and swung around on the end of the pole? She'd had to show him she was right and he was wrong, and look where it had landed her.

'Maren, are you sure –'

She flashed him a smile that was intended to exude confidence but felt horribly brittle. 'I'm fine.' She grasped the door handle, turning slightly away from him. 'You get back down there and start levering.'

'Heaven protect me from bossy women,' he snorted. There was an infinitesimal pause, then in an entirely different tone he murmured, 'You really are something.'

Maren looked up quickly. But he was already striding away. He jumped down off the track. 'Don't get in till I give the word, OK?'

'OK,' she called back, happiness blooming inside her like a flower opening. For a moment she forgot how sticky, dirty, and dishevelled she was.

She waited a few seconds. Then he shouted. 'Now.'

Carefully Maren pulled the door open. The angle made it awkward for her to hold it as she eased her bottom onto the seat then swivelled slowly to get her legs in. Metal groaned and she held her breath. But the vehicle didn't move. She let the door rest against the lock, not wanting to waste time closing it properly. Besides, if anything went wrong ... Stop it. Just concentrate.

Checking that the handbrake was on and the gearstick in neutral, Maren turned the ignition key. The engine coughed once and was silent. Biting her lip, she tried again. This time it caught. She pressed the accelerator, gently revving the engine. The last thing she wanted was to stall.

'Now,' she muttered. 'First, pull the red lever.' She gripped it, feeling her fingers slipping with perspiration. Quickly she quickly wiped both hands on her trousers, then gripped the lever once more and pulled it firmly. It slid forward and slotted into place. What now? Oh yes, first gear.

Depressing the clutch she eased the gearstick over and forward. She took a deep breath, pressed a little harder on the accelerator and allowed the clutch to come up, a fraction at a time. It was all taking so long – too long. How could Nicholas possibly hold the weight?

She closed her eyes for an instant. Forget that. Forget him. Just concentrate on your feet. Don't rush anything.

Maren felt the clutch bite. Holding her feet absolutely still, hardly daring to breathe, she slowly released the handbrake. Gripping the steering wheel with both hands she pressed down a little harder on the accelerator. The engine note began to rise. She allowed the clutch pedal up a fraction more. Nothing happened. She was bathed in perspiration. Her shirt clung, her trousers stuck. Forget that – forget everything. More accelerator and ease up on the clutch...

Her knuckles gleamed white, so tight was her grip on the steering wheel. The Land Rover moved. Maren's heart lurched into her throat. With an immense effort of will she kept her feet steady then slowly, so slowly, she pressed down the accelerator pedal once more.

The Land Rover moved forward an inch, then another. Maren felt the tyre bite on the branches. Then came a slight jerk which she knew must be Nicholas on the other end of the pole.

Her legs and arms were trembling with the strain but she forced herself to keep the pressure steady and even. Another inch, and then another. It was working. The Land Rover was climbing out of the fissure.

Suddenly there was a loud crack, followed immediately by a splintering sound. She gasped, knowing the sapling must have broken. But she kept the pressure steady. The tension in her legs was becoming unbearable.

Slowly the back of the vehicle rose inch by inch, creeping forward and upward over the branches until it was level once more.

She caught a flash of movement from the corner of her eye, but ignored it as the Land Rover crawled over the rutted track, jolting her unmercifully as it crossed the gullies and fissures to climb a slight incline.

As she reached the top she took her foot off the accelerator, slammed on the clutch and brake pedals and heaved back the handbrake. She rested her forehead on her hands and breathed an enormous sigh of relief.

The door flew open and to her utter amazement Nicholas swept her up in his arms, lifted her out and swung her madly round. Maren shrieked and clung on round his neck.

'We did it,' he laughed, his hair flopping in unruly curls over his forehead. 'We did it.'

'Hang on a minute,' she shouted, still breathless. 'What's all this *we*? As I recall it, you were making matchsticks halfway down the mountain. It was me –'

His head came forward and his lips descended on hers, cutting her off in mid-sentence. His mouth was warm, his lips tender, cherishing hers with an aching sweetness that took away what remained of her breath.

Without releasing her he set her gently on her feet. One strong arm encircled her body, holding her close against him. With the other he smoothed back the curling tendrils of damp hair from her forehead, caressing her cheek, her throat, her neck, until her skin sang to his touch and a sigh that was half a sob trembled upwards from deep inside her.

Her hands moved up from his neck to entwine themselves in his thick black hair.

Nicholas's heart thudded against her breast as he tilted her chin, his eyes straying hungrily over her face. 'We must talk, later.'

'Yes.' She was stirred by his tenderness, such a contrast to the savage, contemptuous brutality of the first time he had kissed her.

It was late afternoon when Nicholas finally drew the Land Rover to a halt. The track seemed to simply disappear, swallowed up in the surrounding forest.

'This is it,' he announced. 'We walk from here.'

As they had driven they'd eaten a makeshift lunch of cold sweet potato and fruit washed down with water. Nicholas had been determined to make up for lost time. This seemed strange to Maren, for hadn't he said only the previous day that out here timetables were flexible?

But not wanting him to think she was taking advantage of the changing situation between them, she had resisted her longing and hadn't asked him to stop while they ate.

At the start of this trip she had vowed not to ask for favours. Now more than ever she was determined not to break that vow. But her heart dropped to her boots as she realised Nicholas intended they should start walking straight away. She was battered and bruised. Her clothes were sweaty, mud-stained and torn, and felt as though she had lived in them for a month. On top of that she was indescribably tired.

She clambered out of the Land Rover, pressing her hands to her lower back to try and ease the discomfort that nagged like toothache in every muscle. Nicholas had already unloaded their gear, plus an extra item, a cylindrical canvas bag which he strapped to the bottom of his pack.

He helped Maren on with her rucksack, adjusting the straps until he was satisfied she was as comfortable as she could be under the circumstances. Yet he seemed not to notice her silence or the weary droop of her shoulders.

Handing her the net bag, he tied the sleeping bags onto the top of his pack and hoisted it onto his back. Picking up the medical box in one hand and the machete in the other, he walked round the Land Rover once more, checking the doors and windows.

'Ready?' he asked.

She nodded trying hard to smile, and he led the way into the forest.

Undergrowth was sparse and they walked with barely a sound on a centuries-old thick carpet of rotted leaves.

The trees all around them were immensely tall, with branches and foliage that spread out like the vaulted roof of some great cathedral. Here and there a shaft of sunlight pierced the gloom through a gap in the canopy, and where the sun touched the earth, plants grew and flowered.

Once she got into her stride Maren felt slightly better. At least she was no longer being thrown about like a pea in a drum. And the physical action of walking was loosening her tense muscles.

But she could not dredge up much interest in her surroundings. She simply followed Nicholas, putting her feet where his had been. They climbed for a while, then the ground began to fall and the going was easier.

They had been walking for about an hour when Maren became aware of another sound joining the buzz and whine of insects, and the rustling of the undergrowth as unseen creatures fled at their approach. It hovered on the edge of her consciousness, tantalisingly out of reach.

Nicholas stopped so suddenly she almost cannoned into him. He turned and smiled at her. Putting down the medical box and machete, he shrugged off his rucksack, then helped her out of hers, piling everything in a heap as she watched in bewilderment. 'Are we camping here?'

He shook his head. 'About quarter of a mile further on.'

'Then why have we stopped?'

Nicholas lifted her rucksack off her shoulders. 'Do you fancy a swim?'

Maren jerked round, staring at him as though he'd gone mad. 'Don't tease. It's not funny when you're as tired and dirty as I am.'

Nicholas put an arm around her and led her gently round a rocky outcrop. 'Such lack of faith,' he murmured.

Maren gasped. In front of her was a large deep pool fed by a waterfall that cascaded from a fissure in the mountainside. Though the pool itself was in shadow, the late afternoon sun kissed the cascade, turning it into a ribbon of pink and gold.

Maren turned to Nicholas, her spirits instantly lifted. 'It's beautiful, absolutely beautiful.'

He grinned. 'Then what are you waiting for?' To her amazement, he pulled off his boots and socks, ran down the slope, and dived fully clothed into the emerald water. He surfaced at once, shaking the water from his hair and eyes, his features usually so forbidding, smiling and relaxed in total enjoyment, 'Well?' he shouted. 'Do I have to come and get you?'

Her weariness falling from her like a cast-off skin, Maren tore at her bootlaces, hopping in frustration as one knotted. Too impatient to undo it she wrenched the boot off, tossed them both with her socks onto the pile of gear, and with a shriek of delight dived in after him.

Chapter Nine

'Food's ready, I think.' Maren mentally crossed her fingers as she called to Nicholas. She lifted several sweet potatoes, their skins crisp and brown, from the ashes and rolled them onto a banana leaf. Cobs of corn, steaming and succulent lay on another leaf.

Nicholas dropped another heap of wood by the fire.

'Can I have the machete?' Maren put her hand out tossing her still damp hair back over her shoulders as she frowned at the fish sizzling on the flat stone in the middle of the embers.

She felt the handle slap expertly into her palm, as if she were a surgeon about to perform a tricky operation, and he was her assistant. She smiled but didn't look up, too concerned with getting the fillets off the stone in one piece.

When the fish had been removed Nicholas built up the fire. Sparks leapt into the cool night air and the dancing flames shed warmth and light over them both as he sat down beside her.

Maren sliced a lemon in half, and while Nicholas pulled the skin off the sweet potatoes, she squeezed the zesty juice over the fish.

Dividing the food onto two banana leaves, Maren

pushed one towards him. Please let everything be cooked, she prayed silently. Pretending to settle herself more comfortably on her groundsheet, she peeped through her eyelashes, watching Nicholas break off a piece of fish with his fingers and put it in his mouth. He chewed and swallowed, then took a pit-pit stalk and ate that. When he had taken a large bite off a corn cob and had still said nothing, Maren abandoned her pretence.

'Well?' she demanded.

He looked up, surprised. 'Well what?'

'Is it all right?'

'Why don't you taste it and see?'

Nervously she nibbled a fragment of each item on her leaf. 'It's lovely,' she declared in happy amazement.

'You aren't exactly confident about your cooking,' he observed, eyeing her over a chunk of sweet potato.

'I'm actually a very good cook,' she retorted. 'But I'm one of those women who likes to use a stove, cutlery and the odd pan or two. Luxuries, I know, but one does get used to them.'

Nicholas leaned towards her. 'Be honest, when did you last enjoy the taste of food as much as this?'

Maren shyly flicked her hair back over her shoulder, met his glance and giggled. 'I can't remember. Maybe it's because I'm eating with my fingers, something absolutely forbidden when I was young. It really is delicious.' She scooped up some more fish.

After their swim, during which they had scrubbed their clothes and themselves free of mud, they had changed into dry outfits. Their wet things now hung over a thin branch resting on two notched sticks stuck in the ground on the other side of the fire close to the tent.

The brisk walk to this campsite had warmed them after the chill of the water. They were on a grass-covered spit of land jutting out from the mountainside. Beneath it the stream leading from the waterfall and pool chuckled.

The sun had almost gone down when they'd reached the site. Maren had scarcely had time to admire the panoramic view before Nicholas, ordering her to put the tent up, had hurried down to the stream to catch supper.

She wondered if she was allowing him to order her about just a little too much. Should she submit so readily to his peremptory commands? Yet it did seem the most sensible thing to do. She couldn't catch fish, certainly not without boxes full of tackle.

Nicholas would probably dangle a worm over the water and order the fish to jump out. And the fish, recognising its true purpose in life, would obey. Maren grinned at the mental image.

She could pitch a tent, and it was more sensible for her to cook rather than punishing her hands and exhausting her strength chopping wood. Anyway, if she was really honest, she hadn't the slightest desire to argue or rebel. She had never felt happier or more completely alive.

As she stared into the flames, totally relaxed, her hunger satisfied, she felt herself merging with her surroundings. The chuckling stream, the towering trees, the whispering air cool and night-dark, were all part of her, just as she, a tiny insignificant dot on this fragment of earth, was a part of it.

It was as though the brooding mountains pulsed with a prehistoric life-force. It echoed in the vast dome of the sky, where galaxies of stars tinkled like bells in the endless solar wind streaming from the farthest reaches of space.

'What are you thinking about?' Nicholas's deep voice broke softly into her reverie.

Maren glanced at him, noted his quizzical half-smile, wondered if he'd ridicule her and decided she didn't care.

'I love this country.' She hugged her knees, tilting her head back. The fire cast its warming light over her face and throat. 'Not just for itself, but for what it has done to me. I feel a bit like an onion. As though, one by one, layers of what I thought was me have been peeled away, and I'm learning who I really am.' She bowed her head and her hair curved forward to hide half her face. 'I suppose that sounds ridiculous.'

'No,' Nicholas replied. 'It sounds … honest.'

'But I've only been here, what, four days? Yet it seems so much longer, almost –'

'A lifetime?'

She looked at him quickly. But he wasn't laughing.

'Measuring time in hours and minutes is a typically human invention, artificial and irrelevant,' he said. 'All it achieves is to impose an unnatural stress. People are always worrying about being too late for this, or too early for that. The only sensible measurement is that of nature: daylight and darkness, the phases of the moon, and the changing seasons.'

'Or experiences,' Maren said. 'When I'm old I'd

like to look back over my life and remember it not in years or months, but in experiences. Things I've learned; people I've known. Sometimes a flash of realisation can have much more of a far-reaching effect than a situation that may have existed for years.' She spoke with feeling, thinking of the number of times in the past few days that had happened to her.

'Springtime in England,' Nicholas mused. 'That's something to treasure.'

Was it just the season that meant so much to him, Maren wondered or was it linked to another memory? Someone he had loved perhaps? Maybe still loved?

Before she had time to recognise the disturbingly painful pang as jealousy, he turned to her with a self-mocking grin. 'Probably because I haven't seen it for five years. We English exiles get horribly sentimental about things we either don't notice when we're "at home", or else complain about.'

So there wasn't anyone else on his mind. The cloud on her horizon dissolved like mist in sunshine.

'Snow at Christmas,' she smiled, thinking back. 'I can't ever remember seeing it, but it was always something I desperately wanted to happen when I was a child.'

'Hot cocoa on a winter's night with a gale howling outside.' He raised a challenging eyebrow.

'The smell of freshly baked bread,' Maren sighed.

'Sailing on Saturday afternoons.'

'Wild strawberries.'

'A Chopin nocturne.'

'Riding on Dartmoor.'

'Schooldays.'

'Ugh, no.' Maren grimaced, 'I didn't enjoy school much. My father's job took him abroad a lot. Mother wanted to be with him, but she wouldn't leave us at boarding schools. She was convinced that travel would broaden our minds and expand our horizons. But all I remember are the first days of new terms, not knowing anyone, and being told to "make friends, Sarah will show you around later". Of course Sarah never did. And who could blame her? She hadn't asked to be responsible for the scarlet-faced, tongue-tied bundle of nerves that was me.'

'Did you never go to a mixed school?' Nicholas asked with gentle curiosity.

Maren shook her head. 'Mother said there'd be time enough for *that sort of thing*, by which I think she meant boys, later. Our function was to absorb as much education as possible along with extras like painting lessons, dancing lessons, piano lessons, riding lessons, skiing lessons, elocution and deportment and a cordon bleu cookery course.'

Nicholas's eyebrows had climbed higher and higher during her recital.

'Please don't misunderstand,' Maren said quickly. 'I'm not ungrateful. My mother honestly believed she was giving us the best possible start in life. Lucy, my sister, loved every moment of it. She had a wonderful season –'

'Season?' Nicholas queried. 'Does that still go on?'

Maren laughed. 'Oh yes. Though there's a lot more emphasis on fundraising for charities. But underneath –' She shrugged.

'You didn't enjoy it?

She shook her head emphatically. 'I persuaded my mother that as far as I was concerned it would be a total waste of time and money. I wanted to go to university and study medicine. I spent most of the parties I couldn't get out of in the loo with a book.'

Nicholas's gaze was searching. 'Go on.'

Maren shrugged again. 'Lucy met George –'

'The farmer?' Nicholas enquired with heavy irony.

Maren felt herself blush. 'Well, actually he's a marquis. Yes, he has a farm manager and a land agent, but he's very hands-on about managing the estate.'

'The house is open to the public?' Nicholas asked.

Maren nodded. 'Afraid so. Well, most of it is. They've kept one wing private for themselves.'

'So Lucy met George. Then what happened?'

'They got married the following year and they've been blissfully happy ever since.' Maren heard the wistful note in her own voice and quickly covered it with a bright smile. 'There you have it: a potted family history.'

'What about you? Have you never been in love?'

It was a rabbit-caught-in car-headlights moment.

'Not classified information is it? Top secret? Burn after reading?'

'No.' She glanced away. 'It – I'm just surprised you asked.'

'Why?'

'Well, I …' she shrugged, flustered.

'Not polite, you mean?'

'No, that wasn't – I simply wasn't expecting it, not from y –' she broke off but it was too late.

'Not from me?' Nicholas pounced. 'Why not from

167

me?'

'It never occurred to me that you'd be interested.'

'Well, I am. Now, do I get an answer?'

'I don't know,' Maren hesitated.

'You don't know what? Whether to answer? Or if you've ever been in love?'

'Whether to answer.'

'Ask me.'

'Ask you what?'

'Ask me if I've ever been in love.'

'I don't think I should. It's really none of my business.' But she wanted to. She wanted to very much.

'Ask me anyway.'

'All right. Have you?'

'No.' He moved one shoulder. 'I'm a normal healthy man, with what I'd say is a normal healthy sex drive.'

Maren was glad the firelight masked the blush that was climbing her throat and face. She vividly remembered the powerful urgency of his body on hers and the voluptuous yearning his kisses aroused in her. He would have had no difficulty finding willing partners. Had it not been for her inexperience and the legacy of hurt and fear with which Paul had left her, perhaps she too might have …

She glanced up at him, tossing her hair back in a quick, nervous gesture. She picked up a leaf and turned it over and over in her fingers, studying it while she spoke.

'Once, a long time ago, I thought – I know now it wasn't love. Infatuation, maybe. Perhaps I was in love with the idea of love. But the answer to your question is no.' She paused. 'It was not a happy experience and I've never wanted to repeat it un –' she stopped just in time.

She dropped the leaf into the flames and watched it brown and curl over before flaring in a final moment of glory to a fragile cinder.

'Our experiences can't all be happy ones,' Nicholas said. 'We have to know pain and sorrow, even rage, to appreciate good health, happiness and peace of mind. We need contrasts.'

'True. I suppose it's all a necessary part of growing and learning. But sometimes, because of a bad experience, you make decisions – set your life on a particular course –' She faltered. 'You don't realise that what you thought were your reasons for doing certain things weren't the real reasons at all. I'm not making much sense.'

'I would guess that's because you don't often put your thoughts into words,' Nicholas suggested.

Her brief smile acknowledged the accuracy of his observation. Then she sighed. 'All that wasted time …'

'That is exactly what I meant,' Nicholas raised a finger. 'The fact that you want to change something for the future does not mean past decisions were wrong or wasted. They were part of the learning process, making you the person you are.'

He leaned towards her, his dark eyes searching hers while his left hand smoothed back her hair. Cupping the back of her head he drew her towards him. 'A person who is not what she seemed to be. Who appeared as hard and brilliant as a diamond, but is far more like a pearl hiding inside an oyster.' His lips brushed hers. 'Confusing,' he murmured. 'But totally captivating.'

His mouth claimed hers once more, with gentle but insistent pressure. Maren's eyes closed and her senses whirled under the sweet torture of his kiss.

She knew in that moment the reason for her emotional turmoil; the fear, anger, and nameless yearning that had so confused and bewildered her since the moment she had first seen him in the hotel lobby. She had fallen deeply and irrevocably in love with Nicholas Calder.

The realisation struck her with the dazzling brilliance of lightning. Nicholas must have sensed her momentary shock for he released her immediately. Concern furrowed his forehead as he studied her.

'Something wrong?'

'No.' Her pounding heart made her breathless. 'No, everything's fine, wonderful.' She smiled at him. *Was it?* He knew a lot about her: from observation, from what she had said this evening, and from whatever information he'd gained from Russell.

But what did she know about him? Russell had limited his information to a cryptic remark about them having a lot in common. Having heard Nicholas talk about his feelings for the country and the people, Russell had a point.

But the man himself was an enigma. She knew nothing of his background. On the plane she had asked about his family. Stating that he had none he had insisted they drop the subject. On his own admission he had never been in love. No family, no one close. She had seen for herself how completely self-sufficient he was – a man who lived life on his own terms. A loner.

Was there any room for her? Or was she simply a brief diversion, a passing fancy, as she had been for Paul?

'What was he like?' Nicholas demanded softly, tilting her chin with his index finger, so she was forced to meet his probing gaze.

'How did you –' The question was out before she could stop herself.

'Tell me,' he insisted.

Though shaken by his uncanny ability to read her thoughts, Maren found suddenly that she wanted to tell him, wanted to put the ghost and the past firmly and finally where it belonged.

'He was married. Everyone else knew, but I didn't. He was 26, fair haired, blue eyed, doing a postgraduate year for his PhD. He was clever, witty and very popular with the other female students and the staff.' Maren gazed back down the years.

'I couldn't believe it when he singled me out. I'd never had a proper boyfriend. I fell for him like a ton of bricks. He played guitar and sang. He had a nice voice,' she said calmly. 'Not trained, but he used it well. He also had a wife and child. It was six months before I found out. He didn't tell me. One of his friends did. I was 19. He wouldn't believe me when I told him it was over. Then he cried.'

Maren shook her head. 'Can you believe that?' She shivered suddenly and pulled away from Nicholas. Turning towards the fire she hugged her knees. He didn't try to stop her. She could feel his gaze as she stared into the flames.

She felt as if a weight had been lifted from her

shoulders. It was the first time she had talked to anyone about Paul.

'Those who had known reacted in different ways. Some of the boys were awkward and shame-faced. Others, assuming I was easy, came on to me. Some girls offered sympathy but expected details in return. Others couldn't understand why I felt hurt and betrayed. So, he was married, so what? If he didn't care, why should I? Their references to his wife were scathing. They blamed her for not being woman enough for him.'

Maren shrugged. 'So much for sisterhood. They said I should find another boyfriend, or several; show him what he was missing, go out and have fun.'

'And did you?'

'Did I what?'

'Follow their advice?'

Another shake of her head. 'It didn't sound much like fun to me. I told them I was fine. Then I focused on work.

'Would you like a cup of coffee?'

Maren glanced round. 'You're kidding. Aren't you?' She watched him get to his feet and disappear into the tent emerging seconds later carrying an oval pan with a half-hoop handle. He put the pan on the ground and Maren saw it contained two enamel mugs, one teaspoon, and two foil packets, one marked 'coffee', the other 'sugar'.

'I don't believe it,' she cried. 'You've had that in your rucksack ever since we left Goroka?'

He nodded. 'It's the first thing I pack every trip.'

Maren didn't know whether to laugh or be angry. 'Do you mean I've eaten snake and worms –'

'Not worms,' he interrupted. 'They were larvae.'

'That's supposed to make it better? I've had nothing to drink but water or fruit juice that I had to suck that out of a bottle or my hands. And all the time you had coffee –and a pan. We could have boiled water for washing – and the vegetables. Honestly, Nicholas!'

'You wouldn't have appreciated it half as much then as you will now,' he pointed out, pouring water from the bottle into the pan and crouching to set it on the hot embers at one side of the fire.

'I wouldn't have needed it so much now if I'd known about it at the start,' she retorted, glaring at him as he sat down beside her.

'Smell,' he said, holding the open pack under her nose.

She inhaled and the rich dark aroma of freshly ground coffee made her mouth water. She groaned. 'You are the most infuriating, sadistic –'

'Think for a minute,' he urged, suddenly serious. 'You've experienced a great deal in these last few days. A different country, different culture, different climate, food –'

'Yes,' she agreed pointedly, 'especially food.'

'None of it would have impressed you, touched you, made you so wholly aware, if you had simply flown over it in a helicopter while living in an hotel, eating European meals and observing endemic diseases in a large provincial hospital, would it?'

Maren stared at him. 'Do you mean – are you saying I could have done it that way?'

His gaze was steady. 'Yes.'

'Then whose idea –'

'The point is,' he cut in 'you have learned far more about the country, the conditions, the people, and about yourself *because* of the hardships and the discomfort.'

Maren was silent. She couldn't deny that what he said was true. She had learned more about herself in these four days than she had in the past seven years.

He pushed a mug of steaming black coffee towards her. 'Sugar?'

She nodded. 'Three please,' and grinned impishly at his raised eyebrows. 'If I have to wait four days for a cup of coffee, I certainly don't intend to worry about my waistline.'

His eyes gleamed as he leaned back on one elbow and lifted his mug, letting his gaze roam idly over her. Maren tried to ignore the warmth caused by his scrutiny.

'I don't think any part of your body need cause you concern,' he observed. 'Except perhaps your shoulders.'

'My shoulders?' Maren frowned, sipping her coffee.

'Mmm,' he nodded. 'They're going to become terribly rounded if you don't stop trying to disguise the fact that you have beautiful breasts and are not wearing a bra.'

Maren choked on the hot, sweet liquid, coughing and blushing furiously. Nicholas tipped his head back and roared with laughter. Even as she spluttered and gasped for breath, glaring at him with streaming eyes, she could detect no malice in the laughter. It was a spontaneous outburst of delight. He was laughing *with* her, not *at* her.

Pretending indignation, she tried to hold back a smile. But it wouldn't be suppressed. She started to giggle. Within moments both were laughing helplessly.

'Oh, Maren.' He shook his head and reached out to stroke her cheek with infinite tenderness. 'You're such a strange mixture.'

At once she looked away, afraid he might read the truth. Burningly aware of his touch, she longed to return it, to show her love in words and caresses. But she could not, dare not. The scars of fear and hurt, Paul's legacy, held her back. She could admit love to herself, but not to the man who inspired it. To do that would be to lay all her suppressed dreams and yearnings, all her self-doubt and shyness at his feet. If he should tread carelessly – she curled inside, already anticipating the unspeakable pain of his withdrawal, his irritation at her lack of emotional control. Or, even worse, his pity.

He had admitted that she amused and intrigued him, that there was more to her than he had suspected. But not even by the wildest stretch of imagination could that be interpreted as an indication of love. He had been honest about having affairs but never having been in love.

Perhaps her naïvety and lack of experience were a novelty. But that might soon wear off. Then he would grow bored with the very qualities that now attracted him.

Memories overwhelmed her: the way they had worked together to save the Land Rover, their verbal sparring, his unexpected playfulness, the mountain pool where they had swum fully clothed, then splashed about heedless of anything but the joy of the moment. He had caught her ankle and pulled her under. She had retaliated by jumping on his back, trying to overbalance him. But he had simply crashed sideways into the water and she had been forced to let go.

Then he had seized her in his arms, mock-threatening, but instead had kissed her. Cool water had dripped from his face and hair onto hers. But his mouth had been warm and through the wet clinging shirts, their bodies had burned, moulded to one another …

She swallowed the sudden lump in her throat. 'You never did tell me,' she said, determinedly steering her own thoughts and his attention onto a safer subject. 'What was the latest news of the fighting?'

His gaze was thoughtful. Then emptying the dregs from both coffee cups, he rinsed them with clean hot water from the pan and shook them dry. 'It appears the dispute has not yet been settled.'

'What started it?' Maren threw the fruit and vegetable skins onto the fire.

'Non-payment of a bride-price. The brother of the girl in question had arranged a marriage for her with a member of a Gimi family, a tribal group to the south-west of the Fore people. But there was a delay in settling matters. Meanwhile the brother went to visit relatives in an Awa village. The Awa people are among the best bow and arrow makers in PNG. The bows are made of black palm, and the arrows are heavily carved, have long barbs and are braided with yellow orchid fibre. They are in great demand by surrounding groups.'

'Yes, but what did that have to do with the girl?'

'Relations between the girl's hamlet and a neighbouring one had become strained due to disputed rights over land. The brother, aware that tension might explode into fighting, decided it would be sensible to obtain new bows and arrows. But instead of paying with Bird of Paradise plumes, he offered his sister instead and began negotiating a marriage for her with an Awa family.

Naturally the first prospective bridegroom was put out. Concerned about loss of face he demanded the original arrangement be honoured.

Maren listened with growing amazement. 'What about the girl? Has anyone asked what she wants?'

Nicholas shrugged. 'I doubt it. This is politics.'

'Surely you don't agree with it?'

'My opinion is irrelevant. What is happening here is no different to what has been going on all over the world for centuries.'

'But it's so cold-blooded,' Maren argued. 'That girl is being sold, as though she were a – a pound of tea or something.'

'You think that doesn't happen in our society?' Nicholas's tone was scathing. 'Civilised countries go one better. Our women sell themselves. I don't just mean through prostitution. How often have you read about women marrying a wealthy man 20, 30 or 40 years older only to make a fool of him by having affairs.'

Maren looked at him, taken aback by the bitter contempt on his face.

'Come on,' he said abruptly, getting to his feet and

offering her his hand. 'Bedtime. We've got a long walk tomorrow.' He was making an obvious effort to shake off his black mood. But an undercurrent remained, making her wonder.

Lying on her back in the tent, warm and comfortable in her sleeping bag, she listened to Nicholas's slow even breathing and felt utterly confused. He had been tactful and considerate, allowing her to prepare for bed while he damped down the fire. He had even called to make sure she was in her sleeping bag before entering the tent himself.

In the darkness she had listened with quickening heartbeat as he undressed then zipped up his own sleeping bag, wondering if he'd kiss her goodnight, hoping nervous, knowing even one kiss would be playing with fire.

They were alone on the mountain. It seemed as if they were the only two people left on the planet. Around them the primeval forest rustled and whispered as night creatures stirred. The time, the place and the events of the day had conspired to weave an enchantment around them. Did he feel it too? Surely he must.

He turned towards her, leaning on one elbow. He reached out and with gentle fingers unerringly touched her cheek.

Maren held her breath. Despite her fears she yearned for him, drawn like a moth to a flame. She lifted her own hand and laid her fingers over his. He made a small sound deep in his throat. The moment seemed endless.

Then pulling his hand free, he muttered a harsh

"goodnight" and, turning away, settled down in his sleeping bag, leaving her disappointed yet relieved.

Maren woke once during the night. Lying on her back she was dimly aware of Nicholas turning towards her, then his arm falling across her waist. His breathing was slow and deep, and she realised the movement was entirely unconscious. Yet when she turned her back to him, his arm tightened, drawing her backwards into the protective curve of his body. *Safe.* She sighed, relaxed, and drifted back to sleep.

It seemed only minutes later that he was shaking her awake. Maren opened one eye. He held the torch. It was still dark.

''S too early,' she mumbled, screwing her face up. 'If you think I'm going to start walking in the dark -

Nicholas laid a finger across her lips. 'Shh. Get up, there's something I want you to see.'

Maren pushed herself upright. 'This had better be worth it.' She smothered a yawn as she unzipped her sleeping bag and reached for her trousers.

'There's no time for that,' Nicholas said impatiently. 'Just wrap it around you like a blanket and come outside.' He ducked through the flaps. Maren followed, still yawning, dragging her sleeping bag behind her.

The air struck chill as she straightened up, the dew-laden grass soaking her bare feet. She shivered, suddenly realising all she had on was her shirt and panties. She pulled the sleeping bag around her, bunching the surplus against her chest.

She turned to Nicholas, noting vaguely that he was fully dressed. Looking up, she pushed her hair out of her eyes. 'What –'

He grasped her shoulders and turned her round to face the east. 'Hush. Just watch,' he ordered. He did not release her, but stood with his hands resting lightly on her shoulders.

Maren gazed down from their rocky promontory halfway up the mountain.

Moment by moment the gloom was growing lighter. Maren could see the mountain ranges, dark and sombre. The panorama at her feet was various shades of grey.

Then she sucked in a breath as the first pearly rays of the tropical dawn tipped the ridges with silver. Tall, slender trees, etched black against an opalescent sky, offered their branches in silent homage to the daybreak. The mists filling the valleys shimmered violet, turquoise, lilac and palest pink.

'Oh Nicholas,' Maren breathed, 'it's like the beginning of the world.'

Then, preceded by a blush of deep rose and a honey- gold glow, the sun's fiery rim climbed above the farthest ridge. Dense black shapes were touched by the golden rays and became bushes and shrubs, each leaf and flower fresh and vibrant with colour. The aquamarine sky deepened to vivid blue as the pastel shades of dawn bowed to the harsh brilliance of a tropical morning.

'Well?' he murmured into her ear, 'was it worth it?'

Maren twisted her head to look up at him. 'I've never seen anything like it,' she answered truthfully. 'It was almost too splendid to be just the start of another day. It was over so quickly. Is it like this every morning?'

Nicholas shook his head. 'No, all too often it's raining. But with luck we might be in for some dry weather. The night before we left the hamlet, the men were planning a hunt for cuscus, wallaby and tree-kangaroo.'

'What has that to do with the weather?' Maren asked.

His arms fell from her shoulders. For a moment he seemed uncertain what to do with his hands. Then he pushed them into his pockets. 'They believe hunting and killing those animals brings on a drought. So hunts are restricted to periods of rain when dry weather is wanted.' He rocked back on his heels. 'Superstitious nonsense, don't you think?'

Maren met his gaze, read the challenge in it and slowly shook her head. 'It might appear so, on the surface. But I think the people who have lived here for generations, who know the forests, the mountains and the animals, probably see signs and notice changes that outsiders miss. I'd be very wary of dismissing as nonsense anything the native people do.'

She glanced up at him with a grin. 'You see? I have learned something over the past few days.'

'So have I,' he murmured thoughtfully, his gaze enigmatic. Abruptly his manner changed and he became brisk. 'Come on, get dressed. We've a lot of ground to cover today.'

Within an hour they had breakfasted, packed up and begun walking. They followed the stream down the valley for a while then crossed it using a fallen tree as a bridge. Nicholas took a compass reading then they started to climb through the dense forest on

181

the other side. Very soon Maren was breathing hard and sweating as she followed Nicholas up the steep slope.

There was no wind to move the hot moist air, and only rarely was the spreading foliage, a green umbrella high above their heads, pierced by the sun. The rest of the time they walked in gloomy twilight.

It was easier than Maren expected as there was little ground vegetation. She realised this was due to the lack of sunlight. She looked around her. 'Nicholas, what kind of trees are these?'

He glanced round. 'Mostly hardwoods: ebony, teak, cedar, rosewood and mahogany. Oil palm and cinchona also grow wild here.'

'I read about oil palm being grown commercially in Papua New Guinea. But cinchona wasn't mentioned, which is surprising considering it's the source of quinine.'

'That's because it's cultivated in Indonesia which is almost next door,' Nicholas replied.

All around them the air was noisy with the sounds of birds and insects.

'Listen to that racket,' Maren pulled a face, 'what on earth is it?'

'Cockatoos, parrots – look.' He caught her arm, forcing her to stop and pointed through the trees to his right.

Maren saw a small, plump, long-legged bird with iridescent green plumage. 'What is it?' she whispered.

'A jewel thrush,' he whispered back. But as he shifted from one foot to the other, a twig snapped beneath his foot and the little bird ran off at great speed, darting beneath the herbs and low leaves of plants growing out of the thick humus on the forest floor.

'Wasn't it a beautiful colour?' Maren was enthralled. They walked on. All around her the trees were hung and entwined by ropelike creepers.

'Wait until you see some of the birds of paradise,' Nicholas said.

'How did they get their name?' Maren asked, 'Was it because of their gorgeous colours?'

'No. The first skins imported into Europe had no feet, and this together with their glorious plumage led to the belief that they were not of this earth, but wanderers from paradise.'

'What a lovely story,' Maren smiled.

'Especially as they're related to crows, which are hardly striking,' Nicholas said drily.

'How many different species are there?'

'Forty. But the bower birds are even more fascinating, though they aren't as spectacular to look at as the birds of paradise. It's their behaviour that's bizarre.'

'How? What do they do?' Maren was enthralled.

'They build fantastically elaborate structures and decorate them with flowers, berries, pebbles, shells, bones and insects. That's what gives them their name. Some even paint their bowers with chewed charcoal or fruit. Others plant moss lawns, and build stockades to mark the boundary.'

'I suppose the purpose of the exercise is to attract a female?'

'Not *a* female,' Nicholas grinned. 'As many as possible. Surely he's entitled after all that effort?

Especially as it's the only time the sexes meet.'

Maren sniffed. 'I'd have thought he'd be too exhausted to cope with one, never mind several.'

Nicholas's teeth flashed in a mock leer. 'You'd be amazed what a little inspiration, a little interest, can achieve.'

Hour after hour they climbed steadily upward. Nicholas pointed out a long-snouted spiny ant-eater. Almost hidden by the rotting trunk of a fallen tree, it was feeding on a nest of termites, licking them up with its long, sticky tongue.

Later they caught a glimpse of a tree-kangaroo as it leapt 20 feet at a time between branches.

By the time they reached the ridge Maren was very tired. Though they had both taken frequent sips of water to which Nicholas had added the juice of two lemons, the humidity had sapped her strength and she felt limp and exhausted.

When Nicholas announced they would stop for half an hour to eat lunch, Maren merely nodded and slumped to the ground, trying to fill her lungs with the humid air.

After eating the cold sweet potato, mango and banana Nicholas gave her, she thought longingly of meat. But she said nothing. She knew it was wiser not to eat a heavy meal when they had another long walk ahead of them before they made camp that afternoon. At least they would be going downhill.

In fact it proved more difficult in some ways than the climb. The weight of her rucksack and the net bag of vegetables affected her balance and made her movements awkward. The soft spongy ground put a great strain on her ankles and there were roots and creepers to trip her should her attention wander for a moment.

The delicate, white, lacy fungi which had so entranced her were now ignored. Even the flame-coloured passion flowers and exotic orchids, whose petals of creamy-gold and purple made a vivid splash of colour, no longer had the power to break her stride.

Pushing aside creepers and lianas that hung in loops and coils between the trees had become so automatic that Maren barely noticed them. It was only when Nicholas, three strides ahead of her, suddenly turned and shouted, 'Maren – look out,' that her head jerked up, her hand freezing in mid-air.

The machete whistled down only inches from her fingers. What she had thought was simply another liana writhed and twitched, then fell limp and headless to the ground.

'Tree python,' Nicholas said, picking it up and coiling the now lifeless body over his arm like a rope.

'How long is it?' Maren swallowed hard and suppressed a shudder. If he hadn't seen it – if she'd touched it …

'About 12 feet or so, only a youngster,' Nicholas answered casually. 'Even so, you'd have had sore ribs for a while if –'

'Don't,' Maren interrupted with a grimace, 'I'd rather not think about it.'

'Well,' Nicholas grinned, 'it does solve one problem.'

Maren caught the gleam in his eye and sighed. 'I know,' her mouth twisted in a resigned smile. 'This evening's meal.'

They set off again. This time Maren kept much

closer to Nicholas, touching only what he touched. Fell walking in the Yorkshire Dales had not prepared her for this.

They reached the bottom of the valley, crossing three streams that cut deep into the forest floor, flowing fast and furious as they raced down the valley towards the lowlands and the Papuan Gulf.

They made camp two miles further down the valley. Maren was numb with fatigue and could only nod when Nicholas suggested they follow the same routine as the previous evening. She pitched the tent. He built a fire and cut ferns for them to sleep on.

Then while she prepared the vegetables, he skinned the snake and chopped part of it into small pieces. He put some into the pan with water and a few of the chopped vegetables, and set it on the fire. The rest he threaded kebab-style onto a pointed notched stick which he rested on two other notched sticks stuck into the ground on either side of the blaze.

'We'll take these roasted slices with us. It will save having to catch fresh meat for a day or two.'

Maren waited for her stomach to heave in protest, but to her surprise it did not. Perhaps she was just too tired. Or could it be that her preconceived ideas about 'normal' food and behaviour had been shed along with so many of her other fears and inhibitions?

She was very hungry and the thought of the stew and the roasted snake meat made her mouth water. It did, after all, taste remarkably like tough chicken.

The meal was bubbling away merrily. The sleeping bags were unrolled and laid on their mattress of ferns, and the remainder of the python's carcass had been buried some distance away.

At odd intervals Nicholas had glanced up from what he was doing and gazed into the forest, an intent frown darkening his features.

He walked over to Maren who was shaking a white tablet from a foil strip into her hand.

'What are you doing?' he demanded.

Maren glanced up, surprised at his curt tone. 'It's only my antimalaria pill. This is the seventh day since I took the last one, so it's due.'

Nicholas nodded absently. 'What do you take?' he asked, seeming preoccupied as he scanned the forest around them.

'Sulfadoxine,' Maren replied. 'With the growing resistance to chloroquine it's the best alternative.' She shrugged awkwardly, 'You'd know that anyway since you're probably taking it too.' She swallowed the tablet with a mouthful of water from one of the enamel mugs.

'No, I'm allergic to sulfonamides, so I take pyrimethamine.' She offered him the mug but he shook his head. 'I'll take mine later tonight.' He picked up the machete. 'I'm just going to take a look around.'

'Is something wrong?'

'No, of course not.' He gave her an engaging grin. You stay here and keep an eye on the meal.'

'Where are you going?'

'It's not polite to ask questions like that. I shan't be long,' he called over his shoulder, and strode off into the forest.

Maren smiled ruefully at her own restlessness. She had wanted privacy sometimes, and had resented his questions every time she had tried to slip away on her own.

She tucked the foil strip of tablets back into the plastic box that held her own private emergency kit. Her aunt had put it together when she had first taken up fell walking. It contained sticking plasters of various sizes, a needle and reel of thread, three buttons, small, medium and large, three large and three small safety-pins, an elastic bandage, a tube of glucose tablets and a tube of barley sugars, and a small tub of bicarbonate of soda which her aunt used both for indigestion and blisters.

Maren had never travelled without it. Though she had never needed to use any of the contents, the box, now scratched and battered, had become a sort of good luck charm. It was the first thing she packed whenever she went away from her small flat in London.

So much for Maren Harvey, academic and scientist, she mocked as she pushed the plastic box into the side pocket of her rucksack and rebuckled the flap. Picking up her soap and towel she glanced at the fire to make sure it was safe then walked to the sloping bank about twenty feet away. She followed it several yards downstream to where the bank was less steep and the water shallower and slower moving.

Dropping her towel onto the ground beside a bush, Maren sat down and took off her boots and socks.

Edging forward she dipped her hot, aching feet into the gurgling water. It was blissful. In fact it felt so good that with a quick glance over her shoulder to make sure Nicholas had not yet returned, she stripped off her shirt and trousers and stepped into the stream.

Maren gasped as she sat down, surprised at how

bitterly cold the water was. The stream swirled over her, pummelling her weary muscles, sending the blood coursing through her veins like sparkling wine.

She soaped herself all over then lay back to let the tumbling water rinse off the lather.

She knew she ought to get out and dress. Nicholas would be back any minute. Besides, she was beginning to shiver in earnest. Turning onto her stomach she peeped over the bank, and her blood turned to ice.

Two dark-skinned men, carrying longbows almost as tall as themselves, their faces grotesquely painted and their bodies smeared and glistening with oil, were examining the rucksacks. They pulled out clothes, turning them over then tossing them aside. Even as she watched, a third man emerged from inside the tent, dragging the medical box.

He prised open the lid with the point of an arrow. While they pored over the contents of the box, not once did they lay down their weapons.

Maren was shivering uncontrollably. The icy water, so deliciously invigorating a few moments ago, now chilled her to the marrow. Her hands were turning blue-white as the blood receded from them. They ached so much she bit the inside of her lip to stop herself moaning with pain.

What should she do? She dare not leave the stream. Those men were obviously not friendly. She was naked and totally defenceless. She had no weapon with which to fight. Besides which she was alone and there were three of them.

Yet every second she remained in the water increased the pain in her limbs. Numbness was creeping up her legs. She would not even be able to stand, much less run away if they saw her.

Where was Nicholas? Why was he taking so long? How could she warn him?

Then another thought struck her, almost too terrible to contemplate. What if they had already found him? What if he was lying wounded and senseless somewhere in the forest?

The three men suddenly tensed. Bent over the box, frozen in a half-crouch, two stared to the right of the tent. The third whirled round to face the same direction.

Without a word the one who had discovered the box snatched it up and they melted away into the forest as quickly and quietly as they had arrived.

Maren couldn't hold back the sob that broke from her bloodless lips. The muscles in her calves and the soles of her feet were rigid with cramp and the pain was agonising.

She tried to pull herself up onto her hands and knees but her limbs would not respond to her brain's demands. Her teeth chattered so hard they ached. Hot tears rolled down her ashen cheeks as she crawled inch by inch towards the bank.

It was so high. She would never be able to climb it. Her hands would not grip. Her fingers were curled like talons and she could not move them.

She was beginning to feel terribly tired. If only she could lie down. The water would enfold her, cradle her, and she could stop fighting. Her mind was growing cloudy. Her thoughts seemed to be wrapped in cotton wool. Why was she fighting? There was nothing to fight, nothing to be afraid of. All she had to do was lie down, just relax, let go …

Maren closed her eyes and her head dropped forward. The water's icy slap against her face brought her up with a jolt and she gasped and choked.

Then she heard Nicholas's voice, harsh with concern, calling her name.

Her heart gave a great bound. He was safe. He had not been harmed. She tried to shout back, but though the noise filled her head, all that came from her lips was a groan.

'Maren? For God's sake, answer me, where are you?' There was raw urgency in his voice.

Using the last of her strength she forced her remaining breath out in a half-scream, half-sob. 'Nick–'

She heard the sound of pounding feet, then a muttered curse. Then he was in the stream, the water foaming around his legs as he straddled her, lifted her out and swept her up in his arms.

His face was like granite as he carried her back to the fire. Dropping to his knees he let go of her legs, using his free hand to pull some of the scattered clothing nearer.

With one violent movement he ripped off her wet briefs. Pushing her arms roughly aside as she tried unsuccessfully to cover herself, he dried her briskly and thoroughly with his towel. Her whole body was racked with shivers and she couldn't speak her teeth were chattering so much.

He pulled his thin woollen sweater over her head and managed to get her arms into the sleeves. Then reaching into the tent he hauled out both the sleeping bags. After zipping her into her own, he wrapped his around her like a quilt and lay her down close to the fire.

'N – N – Nicholas,' Maren tried to talk.

Busy with the pan, he glanced up at her. 'Don't talk, just try to relax.'

'B – but the m – medicine b – b – box, they t – took it.'

'Yes, I know.' He moved back to sit beside her, holding a cup half-full of steaming broth. 'I looked in the tent as soon as I got back to see if you were inside. I saw it was missing.' He put the cup carefully on the ground then hauled her up into a sitting position. Still she shook.

With one leg either side of her, he pulled her against him so that her back rested against his chest.

Then he picked up the cup and held it in front of her. 'I'll hold it, you sip.'

Determined not to be totally dependent, she struggled to free her hands from the depths of the sleeping bags and lifted them slowly and stiffly to encircle the cup.

Nicholas placed his own warm hands over her icy ones and guided the cup to her mouth. He would not let her speak until she had finished every drop.

The shivering gradually eased, and her blue-white pallor was driven away by the blood returning to her skin.

She relaxed in Nicholas's arms, half-facing the fire, her knees drawn up. His warm breath caressed her ear and neck as his cheek rested against her hair.

She was blissfully warm. She felt utterly safe and tranquil.

'Are you ready to talk now?' Nicholas's deep

voice murmured close to her ear.

She nodded and settled herself more comfortably. His arms tightened around her and she felt happiness leap. How he had changed. How different he was from the cold, arrogant stranger who had introduced himself that first evening. This man was caring, protective and so gentle.

'Tell me what happened,' he coaxed.

Maren rested her head against his shoulder and described all that had taken place. 'I still can't imagine how they didn't see me,' she shuddered recalling her terror.

'It's over now,' Nicholas soothed, 'you're safe. I shouldn't have left you.'

Maren rubbed her cheek against his shoulder. 'Is that why you went into the forest? Did you know they were around?'

'It was just a gut-feeling. That's why I didn't say anything. There was no point in worrying you unnecessarily.'

'They couldn't have known we'd be here,' Maren frowned. 'So what were they doing in this part of the forest?'

'I'd guess they were part of a raiding party, which means the fighting is still going on.'

'But they didn't take any of our clothes or food,' Maren pointed out. 'Why would they steal the medical supplies? They won't know which drugs treat which conditions. So it's of no use to them.'

'It's possible they have some wounded in the party. They wouldn't be able to get treatment at an aid post without risking jail. Fighting is illegal,' Nicholas explained. 'It's also possible they might sell the drugs to someone who does recognise their worth, who will resell them at a profit.'

'You mean a black market? Even here?' She was more sad than shocked.

'Even here.' He was silent for several seconds. 'I'm calling this trip off. It's too dangerous to go on, especially now we've lost all our medical equipment.'

Maren sat bolt upright, twisting round to face him, utterly dismayed. 'But you can't. Why don't we go after them? They have no quarrel with us, we could –'

'Where do you propose we start looking?' he demanded, cutting short her protest. 'The fighting could be going on anywhere within a radius of 50 miles. No, we're going back. You've coped with everything far better than I ever imagined you would. But the risks are becoming too great.' He scowled. 'Brent had no right to expose you to this kind of danger. I'll be having words with him the minute we get back.'

'That should be interesting, considering he's in the States right now.'

'What are you talking about? Brent is in Port Moresby.'

Maren was stunned. 'But – he can't – you mean he's not in America at a WHO conference?'

'Where on earth did you get that idea?' Nicholas looked surprised. 'He is in the capital for a meeting with the Health Minister.'

Russell had lied to her. But why? Did it mean he had never intended going with her? If so, why had he invited her out to New Guinea at all? Then like pieces of a puzzle everything fell into place. She kept her tone neutral.

'Was it Professor Brent's idea that we went by Land- Rover and on foot instead of using a helicopter?'

Nicholas nodded. 'I had my doubts about the whole thing. Fortunately you proved fitter and more adaptable than I ...'

Maren didn't wait for him to finish. 'But you do your own trips on foot, don't you?'

'Sometimes,' Nicholas agreed. 'It allows me to keep more closely in touch with local conditions. I get to know the people better, and it keeps expenses down.'

Maren's thoughts raced as she tried to work out what it all meant. She looked at Nicholas. 'It's clear you were dragged into this against your will, so what was the favour Russell did for you? It must have been quite something for him to have blackmailed you into accepting my company,' she finished bitterly.

Nicholas's features tautened. 'That is none of your business. No one mentioned blackmail.'

'I did,' Maren flung at him. A deep, slow anger was beginning to smoulder inside her. 'And you're wrong. It's very much my business. I'm the one in the middle of this – this bargain. I know it's connected with your last trip, and I know it involves a woman.'

Nicholas frowned. 'Who –'

'Oh, come on. Give me credit for a little sense. The way you acted when we first met was hardly unbiased.'

How could she bear it? How could she accept that she had been betrayed by the two men who, in their different ways, meant more to her than anyone else in the world?

'When you talked about being conditioned by the past, I thought you meant me. But I see now that you were trying to excuse yourself for jumping to conclusions. Dave Edridge was certainly surprised when he learned I was going with you into the mountains.'

'Maren, wait a minute.' His expression was troubled as he tried to calm her. But she would not listen.

'Even Bilas Kanawe, so helpful, so diplomatic, had a hard time disguising his curiosity about my presence with you.' Maren deliberately moved away, swivelling round to face him. 'Everyone else knows what happened, so don't you dare tell me it's none of my business.'

Nicholas stared at her, his dark eyes suddenly vulnerable. 'All right. Under the circumstances perhaps it's better settled now.'

What circumstances? She didn't have time to ask as, in a cold dispassionate voice, his gaze fixed steadily on hers, Nicholas began to talk.

'My last expedition into the mountains was eight weeks ago. There were five in the party: anthropologist Richard Manston, his wife Julia, a bearer, a cookboy and myself.'

Maren felt fury erupt like a white-hot flame. A bearer and a cookboy? When she had had to carry all her own gear and, at his insistence, do the cooking? She dragged her attention back to what he was saying.

'Manston was in his late fifties. But he was very fit and, despite a leg injury, able to maintain a good pace. Being independently wealthy his work was more an absorbing hobby. He told me that he and

Julia had only been married three years. His first wife had died ten years earlier after a long illness.

'Julia was younger, about 25 and from an aristocratic but impoverished family, very beautiful and very bored. It was clear to me that she wasn't interested in her husband's work. Though he fussed over her he seemed unaware of her restlessness.'

In spite of her anguish Maren found herself becoming absorbed in the story.

'We had been dropped by helicopter to spend four nights under canvas in order to observe funeral ceremonies and mourning rites in a Fore village,' Nicholas continued. 'On the third day we were invited to a sing-sing. Halfway through Julia complained of feeling ill and asked me to take her back to the campsite.'

Nicholas's gaze never faltered. Only the tightening of his jaw gave any visible sign of the tension Maren could feel emanating from him.

'When we got to the site, she took off her shirt and bra and insisted I examine her. She did appear to be in pain.' Bitterness and self-disgust at his own gullibility twisted Nicholas's mouth. 'When I realised what she was up to I started to walk away, to my own tent. She followed me, more or less demanding that I make love to her. I told her I preferred to choose my own partners and that as she was technically my patient it was impossible for me to take advantage of her offer. She became hysterical and tore off the rest of her clothes, taunting me with being impotent or homosexual. Then she attacked me, scratching my face and arms. She had very long nails. I pushed her away. She tripped and fell backwards. When she didn't move I thought she had knocked herself out. I knelt down to pick her up and her husband arrived to see how she was.'

Nicholas brushed a hand wearily across his eyes then returned his gaze to Maren. 'Before I could say a word, she ran screaming to her husband and collapsed in his arms saying I'd tried to rape her.'

Maren gasped and her hand flew to her mouth.

Nicholas went on, 'Manston was obviously upset by the whole business. She was hysterical and insisted on pressing charges. It was her word against mine, and I was covered all over in scratches. It could have meant the end of my career if Brent had not persuaded her to withdraw the charges.'

'How did he do that?' Maren asked.

'He was called in to examine us both. Her examination revealed she was two months pregnant.'

'I don't understand.' A puzzled frown creased Maren's forehead. 'What did that have to do with her dropping the charges?'

'Brent noticed Manston's limp and learned he had been involved in a bad car smash two years earlier. Manston mentioned pelvic injuries but wouldn't elaborate. Brent played a hunch and sent a telegram to the surgeon who had operated on Manston. The answer confirmed what Brent had suspected, that Manston could not be the father of Julia's unborn child.'

Maren let her breath out in a rush. 'So she wanted to have you charged with rape to explain the fact that she was pregnant?'

Nicholas nodded grimly.

'What did Russell do?'

198

'He told Julia what he knew and advised her to drop the charges. He also strongly advised her to tell her husband the truth.'

'And did she?'

Nicholas shrugged, running his hands through his hair. 'Who knows? I had been held on conditional bail since the moment we arrived back in Goroka. They left the country within hours of withdrawing the charges. But in the meantime, the story had spread like an epidemic.'

'That must have been terrible for you. Julia Manston must have been desperate to have done something like that.'

Nicholas's head jerked up. 'Something like what? Having an affair because her husband couldn't satisfy her? Or accusing an innocent man of rape to explain her pregnancy? Isn't your sympathy a little misplaced?' he demanded coldly.

Suddenly Maren remembered what had provoked his confession. All her hurt and anger flooded back. She looked him full in the face. 'I would hardly call your conduct irreproachable.'

He looked shaken. 'You surely don't believe – you can't think I would –'

She shook her head impatiently. 'That's not what I meant.'

'Then what do you mean?'

'You and Russell both lied to me. I've been nothing more than a pawn, a means of settling a debt. I trusted you both ...' Her voice fractured. She swallowed hard, clasping her arms across her chest, trying to contain her anguish. 'I haven't known you very long.' *Just long enough to fall in love with you,*

199

long enough to know that when I leave here I shall be leaving behind part of me. The words trembled on her lips, but she held them back. She would not embarrass him or disgrace herself. Pride was all she had left. He had peeled away all the other protective layers. She would not abandon her pride as well.

'It's my own fault. I've been stupid and naïve. From the day I arrived I believed everything you both told me. I never questioned, never doubted. How you must have laughed.'

'Maren, listen …' Nicholas's expression was deeply troubled, but she couldn't stop.

'I've known Russell since I was four. He's been like a favourite uncle. He always seemed to understand me better than my parents did. It was he who influenced my choice of career. He guided me …' She was talking as much to herself as to Nicholas, trying to make some sense of it all, to understand. Why? Why?

Nicholas caught her arm, pulling her gently towards him. 'Maren, listen to me, whatever you may think, Brent cares deeply about you. I'm sure he had good reason for doing –'

Maren snatched her arm away. 'Don't touch me. And don't you tell me what Russell's motives were. The pair of you have used me. Now you decide to call off the trip and I'm supposed to accept it, just like I accepted everything else.'

Maren kicked off her sleeping bag. Clutching his around her, she scrambled to her feet.

'Well, I've got news for you. I came to this country to get specimens for my research. Nothing has changed that. I intend to get those specimens if I have to crawl over the mountains.'

She took a deep breath. 'So, let me make something quite clear, unless you intend carrying me and all the baggage, I'm not going back.'

Chapter Ten

She held his gaze, meaning every word.

'All right,' he said abruptly. 'We'll get your samples. Now sit down and let's eat.'

Relief and reaction left her weak and shaky. She had difficulty holding the pan steady as she poured the thick stew into the enamel mugs. What if he had refused?

They ate in silence. As far as she was concerned the food might as well have been sawdust. When they had finished eating, both set about their chores without speaking.

As she gathered up the strewn clothing and repacked the rucksacks, Maren was vastly relieved to discover her aunt's box half-hidden beneath the groundsheet. The small box of glass phials containing formaldehyde in which to preserve the collected specimens was also undamaged.

Later in the tent, lying with her back to Nicholas, careful not to touch him, Maren thought over all that had happened since they had met. Their initial suspicion, the rows, the dawning of mutual respect, the way they had begun to function as a team, the shared laughter, moments of closeness and understanding. *And his kisses.*

At first they had been a punishment, revenge on the woman he thought she was. Yet through his lips and in his arms, she had discovered another dimension. Soul-stirring ecstasy had released her from fear and she had soared, a bird riding the wild wind, totally free, yet inextricably bound to him.

For a while she had thought – but she was wrong. Hadn't Paul taught her that men were not to be trusted? She'd been fooled again and could blame no one but herself. But surely some part of it must have been real? It could not all have been a mirage.

Maren shut her eyes tightly against the sudden scalding tears. She was lying beside the man she loved, would always love, and she had never been so lonely in her life.

They were ready to leave just after dawn. Nicholas made it plain there would be few stops. They had to reach the swampy river valley where the mosquitoes bred and get out again as quickly as possible.

Though she had to concentrate on keeping up as Nicholas slashed a trail through the undergrowth, she did occasionally catch a glimpse of the other inhabitants of the forest. Lizards and geckos darted up the trunks of trees, huge snails glided majestically over thick, waxy palm fronds and large beetles with metallic green or copper-coloured wing cases trundled like small tanks over a rotting, fallen tree. She found it strange to see leaves falling, flowers blooming and fruit ripening all at the same time.

As the day wore on the air grew more and more oppressive. The unbroken tree canopy acted like a giant pressure cooker, holding in heat and moisture. The air felt starved of oxygen and both of them panted and gasped as they stumbled on up the mountain.

At five o'clock, just after they had crossed the ridge, Nicholas called a halt. Far below them at the bottom of the steep valley, the river flowed sluggishly southwards.

They cleared a small space in the undergrowth and pitched the tent. With no natural water source nearby they had only enough for drinking. There would be no refreshing bathe tonight.

They tacitly agreed there was no point in building a fire, assuming they could find dry wood, which in these damp, decaying surroundings was doubtful. So after eating her share of the cold meal, Maren climbed exhausted and grubby into her sleeping bag and within moments sank into a fitful slumber.

She woke with a start a few hours later. It was still dark. Peering at her watch she saw the luminous hands stood at two-thirty. Then she heard the rain.

It pattered onto the tent like the scampering feet of tiny animals. It streamed from the tallest trees onto those beneath. It trickled from palm fronds onto ferns, dripping steadily onto the fungi, shed leaves and rotting wood that made up the rich, dank compost of the forest floor.

It was still raining when Nicholas shook her awake just after dawn. They swallowed a hasty breakfast and packed up. The waterproof cape Maren had brought from England proved woefully inadequate, so Nicholas cut slits in their groundsheets and they pulled them on over the top of their rucksacks, leaving only their faces exposed.

The appalling humidity was aggravated by the

waterproofs which prevented any circulation of air to the skin, quickly leaving them soaked in their own sweat.

The prospect of reaching their destination in a few hours kept Maren going. But even the thought that she would soon be collecting the specimens for which she had come so far and endured so much, could not lift her misery.

Nicholas had betrayed her trust. Even though it wasn't entirely his fault, Maren did not think she would ever be able to forgive him. Yet she loved him still and it was breaking her heart.

By eleven the incline was less steep and their boots were sinking into foetid, boggy ground. Still it rained, the drops splashing from the trees onto their faces to mingle with their sweat. Around them the smell of rotting vegetation was sickly sweet. Nicholas beckoned Maren forward and pointed. Several feet below them was a stagnant pool, and clouds of mosquitoes hovered just above the water.

'Let's get it over with and get out. We're running one hell of a risk.'

'There are two boxes in the left-hand pocket.' Maren turned her back to him. 'Can you get them out?'

He passed them to her. Opening the top one, her aunt's, she took out a needle and an individually wrapped plaster. Handing the box back to Nicholas, Maren opened the second one and removed a small, flat, glass dish wrapped in a tissue, and a vial of clear liquid. She handed the dish to Nicholas, who watched her intently.

Taking the stopper from the vial, Maren tipped

some of the liquid onto the tissue and scrubbed her left index finger, then after dipping the needle into the vial she deliberately pricked her finger and squeezed several drops of blood onto the middle of the dish.

'What on earth are you doing?'

Maren glanced up. 'Only the females carry the malaria germ and they're the ones that drink human blood. The males live on plant nectar.' She swabbed her finger with spirit once again and pressed the plaster over the tiny puncture.

'I'll do it,' Nicholas said as she reached for the dish. He handed her the boxes and slithered down towards the pool placing the dish at the edge of the black, oily-looking water. The mosquitoes caught the scent of the fresh blood and the whining grew louder as one after another they dived towards the dish.

'How many?' Nicholas called over his shoulder.

'A dozen,' Maren replied.

Nicholas bent down to pick up the dish and Maren heard his sharp intake of breath as the mosquitoes, driven to a frenzy by the scent of human blood, attacked his exposed face and hands.

Maren jumped down beside him, a slim spray can in her hand. She aimed it at the dish and pressed the button. A fine mist enveloped the mosquitoes, killing them instantly. Then she aimed at the angrily whining insects around Nicholas, pressing the button again and again until the can was empty and most of the mosquitoes had died.

Scrambling back up the slope Maren took the dish from him, dropping the empty can into the box.

'What else do you need?' Nicholas demanded.

'Eggs and larvae. They are just below the surface.'

'I'll get them.'

'It's my job,' Maren said quickly. 'It's the reason I'm here. You're not obliged to help.'

Nicholas's glance was withering. 'What shall I collect them in?'

'There's a wide-mouthed test tube in the box.'

Nicholas picked it up and turned back to the pool.

Maren crouched beside the open box, placing the dish on the ground. Unscrewing the stopper from a slim, two-inch long phial, she carefully picked up a dead mosquito from the dish with a pair of tweezers and pushed it headfirst into the liquid-filled phial, then followed it with another one. She filled all six phials and when she had finished, the tang of formaldehyde hung in the moist air.

Nicholas returned and Maren transferred the minute eggs and submarinelike larvae into other phials.

'That's marvellous.' She smiled up at him. 'You've even got three pupae. The ones shaped like a comma? That stage only lasts three days.'

'We aim to please,' Nicholas responded drily. 'Finished?'

Flushing, she nodded and swiftly repacked the boxes. Then she handed them to him and turned so that he could replace them in her rucksack.

'Right, let's get out of here,' he growled. But instead of following the trail down which they had come, he took a compass reading and struck off diagonally across the mountain.

'Where are we going?' She tried to match his stride, her boots making horrible sucking sounds as she pulled them out of the swampy ground.

'Back to the Land Rover,' he said over his shoulder.

She was already panting in her effort to catch up with him. Perspiration trickled down her back. Her shirt and trousers were plastered to her skin beneath the waterproof sheet. 'How far is it? How long will it take us to get there?'

'About two days,' was the curt reply.

Those two days were a blur of misery and discomfort: stifling humidity, tortured muscles and great welts rubbed across her shoulders and the bottom of her back. They stopped only when it was too dark to see and began walking again at first light.

They ate only cold food and Nicholas made no effort to replace their rapidly dwindling stores except with wild fruit and berries picked as they walked.

But what nearly destroyed her was his relentless pressure to keep moving. He did not nag or bully. Instead he withdrew into himself, becoming more terse and monosyllabic. Even after hours of silence, a remark or question from her elicited no response at all. But he kept walking, hour after hour, mile after mile.

She had no choice but to follow, stumbling along in his wake, trying desperately to keep up. Beneath the thick grey blanket of exhaustion that deadened her thoughts and feelings, Maren sensed something was terribly wrong. He was making inhuman demands upon them both. She knew she was near breaking point. It was only the fear of being left behind in the forest's oppressive gloom that forced her on. She had a horrible suspicion that he would not even notice her absence.

208

Just after three on the afternoon of the second day, they were inching their way up a steep incline using hanging loops of lianas to help them when Nicholas pitched headlong onto his face.

Gasping for breath a few paces behind, Maren did not realise immediately what had happened. She stared uncomprehendingly at the prone figure in front of her, then stumbled forward to help him up.

As she sank to her knees beside him, Nicholas braced himself on hands and knees and staggered to his feet, swaying. He lurched sideways and would have fallen again had he not grabbed a twisted rope of creepers. He clung to it, his chest heaving as he tried to suck oxygen into his tortured lungs.

Maren crawled forward and pulled herself upright, seeing Nicholas's face properly for the first time in eight hours. Shock clutched with icy fingers at her heart.

The hectic flush of fever burned in his cheeks and his eyes were glittering and bloodshot. Maren seized his wrist. Beneath the hot skin his pulse raced.

'Why didn't you tell me?' she demanded, her voice cracked and husky, half-angry, half-frightened. 'Nicholas, you're ill, why didn't you tell me?'

He shook his head, his eyes closing for a moment and pulled his arm free. 'I'm all right,' he mumbled, moistening parched lips with his tongue. 'Got to – got to reach the Land Rover.' Making a supreme effort he let go of the creeper and began to climb again.

'Nicholas, you can't,' Maren almost wept, frightened for them both. She scrambled up beside him.

He stopped, his head lowered as he leaned against

a tall, slender tree. He glanced sideways at her. Fury blazed in his eyes at having to waste precious energy in speech.

'Don't be – bloody fool. Can't stay here. Got to – not far –' and pushing himself away from the tree he took a step forward, then another.

Maren scrambled up beside him, put her hand in his, matched his stride. He did not seem to notice she was there as with painful slowness they stumbled upward. Please God help us, Maren prayed, give us strength. Dear God, I love him so much.

Step by step they moved on. Above them the invisible sun sank towards the western horizon.

An eternity later, Maren realised the incline was levelling out. Now the ground sloped gently downwards. Don't look ahead, Maren told herself, don't think about distance. One step at a time is one step nearer home. She smothered an urge to giggle, teetering on the brink of hysteria. Home? Where was home?

The trees were farther apart. The undergrowth was less dense. A shaft of sunlight pierced the canopy of foliage high above them, and like a spotlight, lit their path.

Nicholas staggered and would have fallen if Maren had not thrown herself in front of him, holding him upright until he regained his balance. His stubbly jaw rasped against her hair. Through his shirt she could feel the fever consuming him.

They could not go on much longer. Maren knew that the next time Nicholas fell she would not have the strength to lift him. What would they do? The medical supplies had gone and they were almost out of water.

The Land Rover must be somewhere near. Not far, Nicholas had said. That had been an hour ago. She had kept to the compass reading so they must be close. They had to be. If they had missed – She refused to think further. One more step.

A bird screeched loudly in front of her, making her jump. She looked up, and blinked. Screwing her eyes up, Maren peered through the trees, hardly daring to believe. Directly ahead was a small clearing. It was the end of the track.

Tears of relief and exhaustion spilled over Maren's lashes and trickled down her face. 'Nicholas, we've made it. I can see the Land Rover. We are almost there.' With his arm across her shoulders, she supported him, half-dragging him the last few yards.

They stopped beside the Land Rover and as Maren released his arm, Nicholas sagged to the ground. Dropping her own pack, she quickly pulled his off and unstrapped the sleeping bags. While she was unzipping and shaking them out, she heard Nicholas groan and looked round to see him lean over sideways and vomit.

She could not ignore any longer the awful suspicion that had haunted her since she'd learned of his high fever.

Catching hold of him under the arms, Maren propped him up against the rear wheel. Then, pulling out a clean handkerchief and the carefully hoarded bottle of water, she soaked the cloth and gently wiped his flushed and haggard face. His eyelids flickered and opened momentarily.

'Nicholas, is it malaria?'

He managed a brief nod. She held the bottle to his lips. He managed to swallow a couple of mouthfuls then turned his head away.

She put the bottle down and began to search through his rucksack, growing more agitated as none of the pockets yielded what she sought. She turned back to him and shook him gently.

'Where are your antimalarial tablets?'

He tried to speak, but his eyes closed and all he could manage was a slight movement of his right hand.

Maren tried his trouser pockets, still nothing. She shook him again.

'Nicholas, please, I can't find them. You need a treatment dose. Where are they?'

He made a supreme effort and croaked a single word. 'Gone.'

Maren bit her lip. Gone? What did he mean? He couldn't have taken them all. Then she realised. 'Were they in the medical box?

Another brief movement of his head, then he leaned over and vomited again.

Panic welled up in her. He was getting worse. Without tests, which were obviously impossible out here, there was no way of knowing which type of malaria he was suffering from, the milder benign or the far more dangerous malignant.

She propped him up against the wheel once more and wiped his face again. Then she rummaged in her own

rucksack and brought out her aunt's box. Tearing off the lid she grabbed her own antimalarial tablets. She was about to rip the foil when she froze. He couldn't take them. He was allergic to the drug they contained. An allergic reaction on top of an attack of malaria would kill him. Yet if she did nothing he might still die.

It was her fault. She had blackmailed him into going down to the malaria-infested valley. He had even taken the dish to the edge of the pool. In protecting her, he had exposed himself to terrible danger. He must have known that missing his regular tablet would lower his immunity and dramatically raise his chances of infection. Why had he done it?

Even while they were in the valley he must have known what was happening to him. Yet he had kept it from her until he collapsed.

She had to get him to a hospital. But the nearest one was in Okapa. That was at least 12 hours' drive away down that appalling track. She might not even get him there alive if she could not bring his temperature down and ease his symptoms.

Maren clasped her head in her hands. What could she do? All their medical supplies had gone, stolen by the natives. Her own tablets were too dangerous to use. Right now she would sell her soul for some of that faithful old standby, quinine.

Suddenly she felt a spark of hope. She scrambled to her feet, staring hard at each of the trees that edged the clearing. Her eyes lighted on one. She reached it in a moment, examining the furrowed, brownish-grey bark through the mosses and lichen.

Maren touched it, feeling its roughness under her fingers. Several months ago Guy had shown her a textbook which had explained a method of extracting quinine from the cinchona tree.

Abruptly, she turned away. The idea was absurd, totally impracticable. She might have found a cinchona tree, but to extract even crude quinine she needed various chemicals. Where was she supposed to find those? It was impossible, hopeless.

Nicholas groaned. Maren looked at him. Your fault, it's your fault, her conscience accused. He had fought the fever that was now racing out of control through his body. He had driven himself on, barely conscious, to reach the Land Rover, their only chance of getting back. No matter how much he had lied, or the dangers to which he had exposed her, she owed him her life. Now she held his in the palm of her hand.

She knelt beside him and pulled his penknife out of his pocket. He was beginning to twitch and shake as paroxysms of shivering gripped him. The fever would break soon and he would start sweating as the malaria parasites developed and reproduced in his bloodstream.

Maren shoved the penknife into her own pocket. Opening the driver's door she threw one of the sleeping bags across the seat. Then, heaving and straining she managed to pull Nicholas to the open door. He was awkward and cumbersome, a dead weight in her arms.

'Help me, damn you,' she wept in frustration as she tried to turn him round.

Somewhere in the fog of his stupor Nicholas must have heard. With Maren's assistance he dragged himself upright then crawled into the Land Rover, collapsing face down along the seat.

Maren pushed his legs in and pulled the sleeping

bag tightly around him. She tucked the other one over the top, made sure he could breathe freely then hurried back to the rucksacks, working out what she needed.

First: the bark. Using Nicholas's knife she scraped the moss and lichen off several thin strips and put them on the ground. Next she placed the two enamel mugs and the teaspoon beside the bark. Now: an alkali. With shaking fingers Maren reached for her aunt's box and took out the tub of bicarbonate of soda. She held it tightly for a moment, blessing her aunt, then added it to the other items.

The next requirement was acid. What did they have that contained acid? The battery in the engine. But that was so full of lead it would be highly poisonous. There must be something.

Maren scanned their few possessions scattered around her. Her glance fell on the net bag. All that was left of the fruit and vegetables were four small lemons. Lemons were full of citric acid.

The final chemical necessary was a solvent. There was only one: petrol. Quickly she hauled the spare can out of the back of the Land Rover. The afternoon was drawing on. She did not have much time.

Measuring the quantities was going to be the greatest problem. She would have to translate everything into teaspoonfuls.

Taking a deep breath Maren began the most important scientific experiment of her life. Counting five teaspoonfuls of chopped-up bark into an enamel mug, she added five teaspoonfuls of water and one of bicarbonate of soda. Using the closed penknife she pounded the mixture into a mush. That would set free the quinine alkaloids.

Next, she added six teaspoonfuls of petrol and stirred the mixture briskly then let it stand. After a few minutes the petrol containing the quinine solution rose to the top. Hardly daring to breathe, Maren poured the petrol into the empty mug, and tipped the bark mush out onto the ground. She repeated the petrol extraction once more.

Slicing two of the lemons in half, she squeezed the juice into the petrol solution and stirred it fiercely. Again the petrol rose to the top. But this time the acid in the lemon juice had extracted the quinine back out of the petrol, which was now useless and could be poured out onto the ground. She did it once more then stared into the mug. It held just over a tablespoonful of crude quinine. Would that be enough to get Nicholas to the hospital?

Maren climbed into the back of the Land Rover. Leaning over the front seat, she manoeuvred Nicholas so that he was sitting upright propped against the passenger door. The strain on her aching muscles made her cry out. Then she poured the bitter liquid into his mouth, holding it closed so that he was forced to swallow. He shuddered violently.

Maren cradled his head in her arms, praying he would not vomit again. The quinine must stay down. She had nothing else. They were dangerously low on water. Once Nicholas began to sweat he would need fluids to replace the amount he had lost. She could not remember passing or crossing a stream on the way up. But once they reached Okapa hospital, the doctors could put him on a drip. She had to get him to the hospital.

Scrambling out of the Land Rover she hurled the rucksacks into the back. She topped up the fuel tank, replaced the petrol can, and took a last look round, making sure she hadn't forgotten anything.

It was almost dark. Maren looked up at the small strip of sky visible above the track. At least it wasn't raining. She climbed into the driver's seat. After tucking the sleeping bags closely around him, and making sure the clothes she had rolled up for a pillow protected his head from the edge of the metal door, she started the engine.

It took her a moment or two to find the lights. Then, clenching her teeth, she turned the Land Rover around and set off down the track.

She drove slowly at first, trying to avoid the ruts and potholes to spare Nicholas. But she quickly realised they would never make it unless she put her foot down. In any case they were both being thrown about so much, going faster could not make it worse.

The journey was a nightmare. While Nicholas sweated and shook, huddled in the sleeping bags, Maren talked aloud to herself and sang every song she could think of to keep herself awake. She risked a glance at him once in a while, not daring to use precious time stopping to check his pulse or his temperature.

With her heart in her mouth she slowed to pass the place where the Land Rover – with her trapped in it – had so nearly tumbled to the bottom of the mountain. Once past it, she jammed the accelerator down again, bone-weary and terrified as they hurtled down the track at breakneck speed.

She stopped only once, to pee. Too frightened and

too tired to seek the shelter of the forest, she walked behind the Land Rover. Her legs shook so badly she knew she was nearing the limit of her endurance.

Back in the Land Rover she drank a mouthful of water and coaxed Nicholas into swallowing what remained. She wiped his sweat-beaded face with her towel and once again tucked the covers tightly around his shaking body. Then, chewing the last two glucose tablets, she restarted the engine and, dashing away tears of utter exhaustion, resumed the journey.

Dawn was breaking as they entered Okapa. Maren followed the signposts to the hospital and pulled up in front of the building. She put her hand on the horn and held it there, her head falling forward on the steering wheel.

The next thing she knew the doors of the Land Rover were open and she was being hauled out. Nicholas was on a stretcher being carried into the hospital by two porters.

'Dr Nicholas Calder, malaria,' she mumbled, swaying.

'All right, miss, we'll take care of him,' announced the young Australian houseman who supported her.

Maren blinked and looked hard at him. Her legs felt like sponge rubber, and she clung to his arm. He was bleary-eyed and had the crumpled look of someone who hadn't had enough sleep for a long time.

He helped her up the step and down the corridor. 'Now, if you'll just wait in here.' He opened the door of a small ante-room.

'No,' Maren's reply was husky, but adamant. 'I'll stay with Dr Calder.'

'Come on now, be a good girl,' the houseman muttered impatiently. 'We've got our job to do –'

'Then get on with it,' Maren turned on him. 'Dr Calder is allergic to pyrimethamine. I gave him roughly 250 milligrams of crude quinine about 12 hours ago –'

'Crude quinine?' the houseman was incredulous. 'What the hell did you give him that for?'

'Because I didn't have anything else,' Maren shouted. 'Our medical supplies were stolen.'

'Where did you get it?' the houseman seemed unable to believe what he was hearing.

Maren took a deep breath, clenching her fists. 'From a cinchona tree. Now will you stop wasting time and set up an intravenous infusion of quinine plus sodium chloride and dextrose. He has vomited twice and the sweating –'

'Just a minute,' the houseman interrupted again as they stopped outside the small room where Nicholas was being lifted from the stretcher onto the bed. A nurse bustled in and began by removing his boots and socks, then took off the rest of his clothes. 'Are you trying to teach me my job? What do you know about it anyway?'

'A lot more than you by the look of things!' Maren leaned against the door, covered her face with trembling hands and took another deep breath. Then, clasping her hands in front of her she looked at the houseman.

'I'm sorry. I shouldn't have spoken to you like that.' I'm a doctor, part of a team working on an antimalarial vaccine. Dr Calder and I were on a research trip.'

The young man beamed. 'Hey, why didn't you say so? That certainly makes a difference.'

Maren forced a smile that barely concealed her impatience. 'No offence intended. I'm afraid I'm rather tired.'

'None taken, none taken.' The houseman reached out to pat her shoulder but thought better of it and scratched his head instead. He turned to the nurse, who had expertly tucked Nicholas into bed. 'Bring an IV set and a 500ml bottle of sodium chloride and dextrose.' The nurse nodded and vanished.

The houseman checked Nicholas's pulse and temperature, watched anxiously by Maren. 'Where've you come from?' he asked her.

'The end of the track, south of the Fore area,' she answered vaguely, watching Nicholas's face. 'Do you think perhaps cold compresses?'

'Yeah, fine, I'll tell the nurse,' he agreed. 'No, I meant, where have you come from this morning?'

Maren glanced up, 'That is where we've come from. We left just after sunset last night.'

The houseman pursed his lips in a soundless whistle. 'You wait here, I'll get the quinine.' Then he vanished.

Maren laid her hand on Nicholas's forehead, smoothing back his rumpled, sweat-soaked hair. With a forefinger she lightly touched his mouth, that sensual, rather cruel mouth that had turned her world upside down. 'I love you,' she whispered, saying the words for the first time.

A sudden faintness made her sit down quickly on the hard wooden chair beside the bed. Waves of blackness washed over her, her legs tingled and her arms were suddenly cold. She was so very tired. She leaned forward, resting her folded arms on the edge of the pillow, close to Nicholas's head. Her eyelids were so heavy. She could not keep them open. She laid her head on her arms. If she could just rest for a minute, until the houseman came back…

Maren jerked upright with a start. The blanket covering her shoulders slipped down her back onto the chair. How had that got there? She turned towards the bed and looked straight into Nicholas's dark eyes. He had been shaved and his left arm lay outside the bedclothes, connected by a tube to the IV apparatus.

'What – how …?' her voice was husky with sleep. She glanced at her watch. Four o'clock? Surely she couldn't have slept for ten hours? She glanced up at Nicholas. He read the question in her eyes and nodded with a gentle smile.

'I've been bathed, shaved, had my temperature and blood pressure taken and you never twitched a muscle.'

Maren felt herself blush. 'You should have woken me.' How long had he watched her? What about the houseman and the nurses? What must they have thought?

Nicholas grinned. 'An earthquake wouldn't have woken you. Anyway, you needed sleep.' His expression grew serious. 'You saved my life.'

'Don't, please,' Maren said quickly. 'It was my fault you caught malaria.'

'Rubbish. I've been incubating it since the last trip. A combination of overwork, stress and missing my weekly tablet triggered off the attack. It would probably have developed even if we hadn't got your specimens.'

Maren felt a great burden of guilt fall from her. 'How –how are you feeling?'

'I'm fine, a bit weak, but I'll be up and about tomorrow.'

Maren couldn't hide her alarm. 'Isn't that rather soon? Are you sure – I mean, do you know what type?'

'Benign,' he reassured her. 'Caused by *plasmodium vivax*. I caught it the first year I was out here and I've had a couple of relapses since then.'

'Oh,' Maren nodded, relief coursing through her. She avoided his glance, oddly shy. There was something in his eyes, in his expression, she had not seen before.

'But you didn't know that, did you?' he murmured. 'Macready, the houseman, told me you prepared crude quinine from cinchona bark. And after dosing me you drove for 12 hours to get me here, is that true?'

Maren nodded diffidently, 'I – I was terrified.' She looked down at her filthy shirt and trousers, her scratched and grubby hands. Automatically she raised one to her hair. It felt like a bundle of string, half-in half-out of the ponytail. What a sight she must look.

'Maren.'

She raised her eyes.

'You're the bravest woman I've ever known.'

She stared at him. 'No, no I'm not brave,' she said quickly. 'I was frightened to death the entire time. I talked to myself and sang and cried. I really wasn't at all brave.' He had to know the truth. She couldn't pretend to be a heroine. She didn't feel like one. She felt weak and vulnerable.

The door opened and Macready peered round it. 'Ah, good. You're both awake. Got a visitor for you.' He opened the door wider and Bilas Kanawe stepped into the room, immaculate in white shirt and shorts, a beaming smile splitting his face.

'How truly glad I am to see you both.' The smile vanished. 'Naturally, I deeply regret the unfortunate circumstances.' Then, like the sun emerging from behind a cloud it returned. 'But you are both safe and recovering from your ordeal.' He turned to Maren. 'May I say how honoured I am to have made the acquaintance of a lady as brave and resourceful as yourself.'

'Please,' Maren interrupted, embarrassed by the compliment. Bilas Kanawe merely made an impeccable bow and continued. 'No doubt you will wish to return to your hotel to change and recuperate. I have a helicopter waiting for you.'

Maren was startled. She glanced at Nicholas who was still watching her. 'But – but the Land Rover. What about my rucksack ?'

'All is taken care of,' Bilas said proudly. 'Dr Calder's things remain here. Yours are already in the helicopter. Come.' He offered his arm.

Maren bit her lip. There was no further reason to stay. She did desperately need a bath and change of clothes. Nicholas was in safe hands and recovering, she had her specimens, the trip was over.

Swallowing a lump in her throat, Maren turned to Nicholas and extended her hand. 'G-goodbye, Dr Calder.' She struggled to keep her voice steady, taking refuge in formality. 'It has been an experience

I will never forget.' Hadn't Russell said those words over the telephone the day she had arrived? *An experience she would never forget.* He could not possibly have known how prophetic they had been.

Nicholas's hand closed around hers and their eyes met, locked.

Bilas cleared his throat politely, 'The helicopter is waiting,' he reminded her.

Still holding Maren's hand, Nicholas glared at him. 'Damn your efficiency, Bilas. Go and sit in the blasted thing yourself. Fly around in circles if you like. But get out of here. You too, Macready.'

Bemused by this sudden unexpected reaction, both men instantly retreated.

'And close the door,' Nicholas shouted after them. He lay back on the pillow looking up at Maren. 'Don't go,' he said softly, urgently. 'Stay here with me.'

Maren stared at him, wide-eyed. 'But – but the specimens …' she stammered, saying the first thing that came into her head.

'Bilas can put them on a plane to England,' Nicholas said impatiently. Then his features grew taut. 'Don't go.'

Maren didn't know what to say. Desperately needing time to think she pulled her hand free. Clasping her arms tightly around her body she turned to look out of the window, in an agony of indecision. He wanted her to stay, but as what? His assistant? A purely professional arrangement? But how could she, loving him as she did.

Sooner or later she would betray herself and it would all explode in her face.

She stared at the forested slopes, remembering vividly the danger and discomfort she had faced. But that paled into insignificance compared to the anguish of loving him, and the choice she had to make.

'It's all right,' he said, his deep voice harsh with an emotion she could not identify. 'I quite understand. You don't have to say anything.'

She spun round.

He smiled crookedly. 'Do you remember when I told you to use my full name, that "Nick" was only for my friends? I knew then you could never be just a friend. It had to be all or nothing for us.'

Maren's heart lurched. What was he saying?

Nicholas laughed. It was a raw tearing sound. 'Ridiculous, isn't it? The first time I fall in love, and I blow it.'

'Love?' Maren croaked. 'Me?'

A kaleidoscope of expressions chased across his gaunt face. Then with a "what-the-hell" shrug he nodded.

Maren couldn't move. Her eyes brimmed with tears and a smile of pure joy parted her lips.

Nicholas frowned, then she watched hope dawn. 'You don't mean … you too?'

She nodded and stretched out her hand to him.

Nicholas pulled her down onto the bed and with his free arm held her tightly against him, possessing her mouth with a fierce hunger that demanded response. She gave it willingly, joyfully, feeling the thunder of his heart against her breast.

They broke apart, breathless and trembling. 'God, I've wanted – I've waited so long for you,' he murmured, kissing her eyes, her lips, her throat, as though he could not get enough of her. Burying his fingers in her tangled hair, he tugged her head back. 'You are sure? You've got to be sure,' he grated. 'I lost my parents and my kid brother in a car smash when I was ten. My grandmother took me to live with her. I adored that woman. She died of a heart attack, on the kitchen floor as I held her in my arms. I was 15 years old.'

Maren watched Nicholas relive the tragedies that had marked him, and ached to comfort him.

'After that I swore I would never allow myself to love anyone, ever. Love meant loss and pain, and I'd had enough to last a lifetime. So you'd better be sure, Maren.'

She gazed at him, her face tear-streaked and glowing, her eyes offering her heart and soul. 'I'm sure I knew the moment I saw you. But I didn't recognise it then. Oh, Nicholas, I love you so much.'

'When will you marry me?' he demanded, holding her close.

Maren dimpled. 'As soon as you're free of that thing.' She nodded at the IV apparatus.

'Go and call Macready,' Nicholas growled. 'We're getting out of here now.'

Maren's gurgling laughter echoed down the corridor.

One week later, brimming with happiness, she stood at the entrance to the little mission church. The man at her side patted her hand as it rested on his arm.

'You look ravishing, my dear. Not exactly a traditional gown, but as beautiful as the person wearing it.

Maren looked down at the sleeveless butter-yellow dress that fell in tiers from the rounded neckline to her feet, caught at her waist by a belt of green, gold and bronze beads. Her glossy hair, curling softly on her shoulders, was held behind her ears by two creamy-gold orchids matching those in her bouquet.

She smiled at him, 'I think I look very traditional – for Papua New Guinea. One thing still puzzles me, though. Why weren't you surprised?'

Professor Russell Brent's eyebrows lifted. 'But why should I have been? Didn't I say you had a lot in common? All you needed was the chance to realise it.'

They exchanged a long look. 'Ready?' he asked.

'Ready,' Maren replied. And they walked down the aisle to where Nicholas waited.

Accent Amour

More **Dana James** from **Accent Amour**

www.accentpress.co.uk